Preface

In a world where art imitates life, the lens of
a camera can reveal both the beauty and the
tragedy hidden within human existence. It
can immortalize a fleeting moment or distort
reality, blurring the line between what is
authentic and what is imagined. The Final
Cut is not a book about filmmaking or the
pursuit of artistic achievement—it is a story
about control, obsession, and the devastating
consequences of seeing life only through the
eyes of a voyeur.

Mike, the protagonist, starts his journey with
a seemingly innocuous hobby: capturing his
wife's candid moments on camera. But as
his fascination grows, so does his need to
orchestrate her every move, turning what
could have been a window into their shared
experiences into a one-sided spectacle of

dominance. When tragedy strikes and he relocates to the neon-lit streets of Bangkok, the allure of creating a film with a new muse entices him to cross boundaries he never imagined.

What begins as an attempt to preserve fleeting beauty turns into a chilling exploration of exploitation and manipulation. Each scene Mike directs becomes a piece of a much larger, more sinister puzzle, drawing him—and his unsuspecting subjects—further into darkness. Through Mike's journey, The Final Cut delves into the heart of human vulnerability, exposing the dangers of unchecked power and the allure of pushing the limits of one's own morality.

This story may disturb, provoke, and raise difficult questions about the ethics of creativity and consent. But ultimately, it serves as a stark reminder of how easily art can slip into cruelty when it loses sight of humanity. It is a tale about a man who not only loses himself in the pursuit of a perfect shot but destroys the lives of those who become unwitting characters in his self-destructive masterpiece.

As you read this book, consider the roles we play, the stories we create, and the unseen impact of observing rather than participating. This is a story where every frame is both an illusion and a revelation, and where the camera doesn't just capture life—it consumes it.

The Final Cut

Table of Contents

Chapter One: The wife

The woman knelt on the cool tiles of the shower room, her body moving in slow, mechanical motions as she scrubbed the floor. Her slim frame, just shy of 60 kilos, seemed even lighter as if the weight of her thoughts were all that kept her anchored to the ground. Long black hair, streaked with strands of silver, fell over her face as she worked, hiding the weariness in her deep brown eyes. She was 5'4", with a posture that once radiated elegance, pride—beauty that could stop men in their tracks—but now it seemed burdened, as if the air itself pressed heavily on her.

In her late 40s, she still carried the grace of her younger years. She was once the heartbeat of Bangkok's social scene—the "party girl," as they had called her. Mingling with the city's 'HiSo'—the high society people who flocked to her for her charm, her beauty, and the way she seemed to float effortlessly through every exclusive party, every private event. She had been invited everywhere, desired by everyone. Yet, here she was, half a world away from that life, on her hands and knees in a small house in England.

The sunlight streaming through the window made the day seem almost too beautiful, as if mocking her. It was a Monday afternoon. The kind of day she once would have spent shopping at Bangkok's finest boutiques, surrounded by luxurious silks and perfumes, the soft click of her high heels on the pavement echoing with confidence. But those days were far behind her. Now, she wore a loose white T-shirt and black pants, her attire as plain and dull as her spirit had become.

Her hands were red from the scrubbing, rough from years of hard work she never thought she'd have to endure. Life had changed—so drastically, so painfully—that sometimes she couldn't remember who she used to be.

Depression had long ago wrapped its cold fingers around her mind, dragging her into depths that were dark and unrelenting. The scars on her wrists, hidden beneath the sleeves of her shirt, were a testament to the battles she fought, and lost, more often than she cared to admit. She had tried, more than once, to end it all—to stop the ache that lived inside her. She had failed, every time, only to wake up again in the same prison, in the same body she no longer recognized.

Now, all that remained was this. The cleaning, the mundane tasks that kept her moving, kept her from drowning in her own thoughts. She scrubbed, the rhythm of the work almost hypnotic, her mind wandering to memories she could hardly bear. She could see it all so vividly—Bangkok, the lights, the parties, the laughter. She had been surrounded by wealth, by beauty, by excitement. She was always at the centre of it. But where had that taken her?

Her hands paused for a moment, the scrubbing slowing to a stop as she sat back on her knees. The silence of the house closed in around her. It was suffocating. She glanced at the small window, at the sunlight pouring in. She could almost feel its warmth on her skin, could almost taste the freedom of the outside world. But there was no escaping this reality. No money, no friends, no escape. Only this—this small, stifling house in a foreign land, where she felt more a prisoner than she ever had in the vibrant streets of Bangkok.

Her eyes filled with tears, though she didn't let them fall. Crying had become something she rarely allowed herself anymore. It didn't help. Nothing did.

Chapter Two: The Husband

Mike sat on the edge of the worn leather armchair, the smell of old tobacco and whisky soaked into its creases. His short grey hair, once thick and dark, now thinned with age, was cropped close to his scalp. His face, deeply etched with the lines of time and wear, spoke of years lived in excess, of nights that blurred into mornings, and of pleasures that had long since lost their charm. He stared absently out the window, watching the sunlight filter through the leaves of the old oak in their garden. It was a far cry from the view he used to have.

The town he lived in now was the one he had been born and raised in. A small, unremarkable place in the English countryside where the days drifted by in quiet monotony. It was nothing like the chaotic, pulsing streets of Bangkok where his life had once been a whirlwind of indulgence. He had grown up here, knew every cobblestone and corner shop, but after a few years of steady work and failed relationships, something inside him had yearned for more. That yearning had pulled him to Thailand, and once there, he had fallen deep into the clutches of its nightlife.

He'd spent over a decade in Bangkok, living like a king among the expats, the rich tourists, and the local girls who knew how to keep men like him coming back night after night. He'd spent his money freely, recklessly. On any given evening, he'd drop

20,000 to 30,000 baht like it was pocket change. It was easy to do on Sukhumvit Road, where the bars and clubs lined the streets in neon invitations. He had known every corner of the city, every place worth knowing. His apartment on Soi 13 had overlooked the sprawling chaos of Bangkok, a city that never slept, never slowed. From his window, he could watch the lights flicker across the skyline and feel the thrum of life below.

It was in one of those bars, down the street on Soi 11, where he had first met her.

She had been different then. Vivacious, magnetic. She'd stood out even in the crowd of beautiful women, with her long black hair cascading down her back and her eyes sparkling with mischief. She was a force of nature, always surrounded by the movers and shakers of Bangkok's nightlife. The party girl who danced through the nights, always in the company of the city's elite. He had been drawn to her instantly. Something about the way she carried herself, her effortless charm, her laughter that cut through the noise of the bar. She had made him feel alive in a way he hadn't in years.

At first, she had been just another thrill. Another beautiful woman in a city full of them. But as the months went by, something had shifted. He had fallen for her, deeply. And when the time came for him to leave Bangkok, to return to the quiet town he had once called home, he couldn't imagine going without her.

He had promised her a new life. He had promised her love and security, a future far away from the dizzying streets of Bangkok. But now, years later, he could feel the weight of those promises pressing down on him. The life he had given her was not the one she had been made for. He knew it, even if he didn't say it aloud.

The woman who used to light up the night now spent her days cleaning the house, trapped in a routine as stifling as the quiet English air that surrounded them. She had become a ghost of her former self, and in a way, so had he.

Mike shifted in the chair, the leather creaking beneath him. He ran a hand over his face, feeling the roughness of his stubble. His skin was weathered, his eyes dull with the fatigue of a man who had lived too hard for too long. In his sixties now, he wasn't the man he used to be. He had left the party life behind, but not without consequence. His body ached, his mind often wandered, and some nights he found himself longing for the rush of the Bangkok streets. The laughter, the heat, the intoxicating energy of it all. But those days were gone.

He had chosen this life, this quiet existence, thinking it would be enough. But looking at her now, at the sadness that seemed to cling to her, he wondered if they were both prisoners of the choices they had made. She, trapped in a house far from home, and he, trapped in the memory of the man he once was.

He closed his eyes, leaning his head back against the chair, the sunlight warming his face. Somewhere deep inside, he felt a flicker of guilt. For what, he wasn't entirely sure. Maybe for taking her away from the life she knew. Maybe for dragging her into his own emptiness. Or maybe it was for not being able to give her the life she deserved, the life he had promised all those years ago in a bar on Soi 11.

The house was quiet, the only sound the distant hum of cars passing by on the road outside. He sighed, his chest heavy, as the memories of Bangkok swirled in his mind like smoke from a dying fire.

Chapter Three: First meeting

The bar on Soi 11 was alive with its usual buzz, the air thick with the scent of perfume, cigarettes, and spilled liquor. It was the kind of place where the nights bled into mornings, where laughter was loud and inhibitions were left at the door. Mike sat at his usual spot, a corner booth that gave him a clear view of the entire room. His night had already begun, and he was surrounded by a small huddle of girls, each one vying for his attention. He wore his charm loosely, tossing out drinks like confetti, his eyes scanning the room as if it were all a game.

This was his routine—every night the same. He'd buy drinks, flash some cash, and when the time felt right, he'd pay the bar fine for a couple of girls, whisking them off to the next adventure. The clubs, the after-hours joints, the nights that never seemed to end. He was well-known here, the regular expat who had fallen in love with Bangkok's intoxicating nightlife. The Mama San, the woman who managed the girls, adored him. Mike had a way of making people feel special, especially when he showered them with gifts. Just last month, he'd bought her a Rolex, a token of his affection that kept him in good standing at the bar. She always made sure he had the best seat, the best company.

Tonight felt no different. The drinks flowed freely, and the girls giggled at his jokes, leaning in closer with each passing minute.

Mike soaked it all in, the easy pleasure of the moment. But then, something caught his eye. The music had changed, a familiar bass line thumping as the DJ spun another track, and that's when he saw her.

She walked in with the DJ, a friend, as he later found out, but at that moment, all he could think about was how she seemed to light up the room without even trying. Minow. Her long black hair fell effortlessly down her back, her skin smooth and glowing in the dim light. She moved with a quiet confidence, not like the other girls, whose eyes flicked toward men like Mike the second they walked in. She didn't seem to care who was watching her. And yet, he couldn't stop watching her.

His eyes followed her as she made her way to the bar, her laugh soft but distinct above the music. There was something about her— an elegance, a self-assuredness that made her stand out from the crowd of girls who were always eager to please. For a moment, Mike was at a loss. She wasn't like the women he usually entertained, but that only intrigued him more. He had to talk to her.

His usual bravado kicked in as he signalled the Mama San, who quickly leaned in, flashing him a smile. "Who's the new one?" he asked, nodding toward Minow.

"Her name is Minow," she said with a knowing look. "She's not like the others, Mike. Be careful."

He smirked. "I like a challenge."

He rose from his seat, leaving the other girls behind with barely a second thought. He moved across the room with practiced ease, sliding into the seat next to her at the bar. She glanced up at him briefly before turning her attention back to her drink, a signal that any other man might have taken as disinterest. But Mike wasn't just any man. He had never met a woman who didn't eventually give in to his charm, to his money.

He leaned in slightly, flashing the same grin that had worked a thousand times before. "How much?"

It was his line. The line. The one he always used, the one that opened doors and loosened conversations. It was crass, but it always worked. Until tonight.

Minow froze, her expression tightening as she processed his words. She turned slowly, her eyes narrowing, and for the first time since he'd walked into that bar all those years ago, Mike felt the weight of rejection. Pure, cold rejection.

"Excuse me?" she said, her voice cool and sharp, like a knife cutting through the haze of alcohol and ego that surrounded him. Her face, which had mesmerized him only moments before, was now clouded with disgust. She shook her head, her lips curled in disdain.

"How much?" he repeated, more out of reflex than understanding. It had always worked, hadn't it?

But Minow wasn't one of the girls who lived on the fringes of Bangkok's nightlife, waiting for the right price to be named. She didn't belong to the world Mike had wrapped himself in so comfortably. Her eyes flared with anger, and without another word, she stood up, turning her back on him.

The moment was swift, but the impact hit Mike harder than he'd ever admit. She walked away, leaving him standing at the bar, the music pulsing around him as if the world hadn't just shifted in a way he couldn't explain.

For the first time in years, Mike felt…unsettled. He watched as she rejoined the DJ, her laugh soft as before, but now it was distant, out of reach. Something stirred inside him. It wasn't lust, or the thrill of the chase. It was something deeper, something he couldn't quite name.

He watched her from across the room, that proud figure moving so gracefully through the crowd, and something in him shifted.

This wasn't a game. This wasn't like the other nights. She wasn't like the other girls.

For the first time since he'd set foot in Bangkok, Mike didn't feel like the king of the night. He felt like the fool.

Chapter Four: Phone number

The night was winding down, and the once-lively bar had taken on a softer, slower energy. The DJ was still spinning tracks, but the crowd had thinned, leaving only a few stragglers lingering over their drinks. Minow stood at the edge of the room, her eyes scanning the scene as she prepared to leave. She could feel the exhaustion setting in, the weight of her circumstances hanging over her like a cloud.

Her friend, the DJ, nudged her as he packed up his gear. "You sure you're not interested in that guy? The 'Farang'?" His voice was teasing but had an edge of seriousness to it.

Minow frowned, remembering the arrogance in Mike's eyes when he had asked her how much. She wasn't just another girl to be bought and sold, and the way he had approached her made her skin crawl. "No, I'm sure," she said firmly, glancing over her shoulder to see Mike still sitting at the bar, a drink in hand, his face shadowed in the low light.

But the DJ wasn't letting it go. "Look, I know he was a jerk. But guys like him? They've got money. And right now, you need that, don't you?" He didn't sugarcoat it. He never did. They'd known each other for years, long enough for him to see through the façade she wore in public—the one that said she was still the queen of the scene. The truth was, Minow had hit rock bottom. Her last relationship had ended in disaster, leaving her not just emotionally drained but financially broken.

She bit her lip, hating how right he was. The savings she had once had were gone, spent on trying to salvage her life after everything had fallen apart. And now, she was at the end of her rope.

Her friend saw the hesitation in her eyes and pressed further. "What's the harm in giving him your number? It's just a number, Minow. See what happens. Worst case, you block him later. Best case... who knows? Maybe you'll get something out of it."

She sighed, looking down at her phone as if it could offer her some kind of answer. She didn't like the idea of it. But she liked the idea of being broke even less. Her pride had carried her this far, but pride didn't pay the bills.

With a small nod, she gave in. "Alright," she said quietly, more to herself than anyone else.

The DJ grinned, satisfied. He called over one of the waitresses and sent her to Mike's table, where he sat nursing his drink. A minute later, Mike glanced up, surprised to see the girl approaching with Minow's number scrawled on a napkin. He looked across the room, catching Minow's eyes just before she turned away, grabbing her bag to leave with her friend.

The next day, Minow almost forgot about the number she had given. She had expected Mike to be just another face in the crowd, a man who would forget about her by morning. But as she sat in her small apartment, sipping on her morning tea, her phone buzzed. She glanced at the screen, not recognizing the number. Her stomach tightened, and for a second, she debated whether to answer at all.

But something in her—the desperation, the curiosity—made her pick it up.

"Sawadi ca," she greeted, her voice smooth and polite, masking her discomfort.

"Hi, Minow?" It was him. Mike. His voice was deeper than she remembered, less cocky now, more... measured.

"Yes," she replied cautiously.

"I was wondering if you'd like to go to a concert in a couple of days. Eric Clapton.

I've got tickets," he said, his tone casual, as if they had known each other for years. There was a pause, and she could almost hear the grin in his voice. "I figure a woman as classy as you would appreciate some good music."

Minow grimaced slightly, thankful he couldn't see her face. She had never been a fan of Eric Clapton, and the idea of spending an evening with Mike didn't exactly thrill her. But she also wasn't in a position to turn down a potential opportunity, however it came.

"Sure, why not," she answered, her voice clipped but polite. "That sounds nice."

"Great! I'll pick you up around seven. I'll text you the details." His voice was laced with enthusiasm, and for a brief moment, Minow almost felt guilty for her lack of excitement. Almost.

"Okay, see you then," she said quickly, not wanting to drag the conversation out any longer. As soon as he responded, she hung up, staring at her phone in disbelief.

What had she just agreed to?

Her fingers tapped restlessly against the edge of her tea cup. She'd expected never to hear from him again. She had walked out of that bar, disgusted by his crude opening line, fully prepared to forget he even existed. And yet, here she was, agreeing to see him again.

She set her cup down and sighed. It wasn't about liking him. It wasn't even about giving him a chance. It was about survival. She needed money, needed a way out of the mess her life had become, and if this wealthy, slightly obnoxious foreigner could provide that, maybe she could tolerate an evening of Eric Clapton.

But as she stood up and paced her small apartment, something deeper stirred inside her. The thought of letting her guard down again, of getting involved with anyone, made her stomach churn. She had been burned too many times before. Men always wanted something, and Minow had learned that the hard way.

She shook her head, pushing the thoughts away. It didn't matter. It was just one night. One concert. One chance to maybe, just maybe, turn her luck around.

But deep down, she didn't expect much. Not from Mike, and certainly not from herself.

Chapter Five: Clapton Concert

The air inside the arena buzzed with anticipation. The crowd was a mix of expats and locals, all gathered to see Eric Clapton, "Slowhand" himself, live on stage. The lights dimmed, and the unmistakable first chords of "Layla" filled the space, sending ripples of excitement through the audience. Mike sat quietly in his seat, already feeling like the night had taken a strange turn.

He glanced over at Minow, who had spent most of the evening mingling with a group of well-dressed Thais at the far end of the arena. It hadn't taken long for her to gravitate toward them the moment they'd arrived. As soon as they passed through the gates, she was waving, smiling, calling out familiar greetings to people in the crowd.

"Sawadi ca!" Minow had greeted half a dozen people before they even found their seats, her voice warm and lively in a way Mike hadn't seen before. They were HiSo—Bangkok's elite. The kind of crowd Minow used to roll with, the kind who could drop millions on a luxury car without blinking. Mike watched, feeling more like a spectator than her date as she was enveloped into their circle with effortless grace.

He sat in his seat, awkward and alone, trying to focus on the music while Minow floated around the arena like she belonged there, far away from him. Clapton's fingers danced over the strings, each note soulful and precise, but Mike was too distracted to enjoy it. He felt out of place, like he'd made a mistake by bringing her here.

Every time he looked up, she was laughing, leaning into whisper something to one of her friends, her face lighting up in a way it never did when she was around him. He wasn't jealous—not exactly. It was more a sense of embarrassment. He had dragged her here thinking it would be a grand gesture, that maybe she'd warm to him if they shared a special evening. But instead, she had spent the night as far away from him as possible.

He couldn't blame her. He knew, deep down, that his world and hers didn't fit together. He'd never dated a Thai woman like Minow before—never bothered with the HiSo crowd, always preferring the company of the girls who hung out at bars like the ones on Soi 11. The ones who never asked questions, who were always happy to drink on his tab and go where the night took them. But Minow wasn't like them, and tonight had only made that clearer.

The night dragged on, and by the time Clapton was winding down his encore, Mike was already counting the minutes until it was over. He was relieved when the final note played, the crowd erupting into applause as the house lights began to rise. Minow had drifted back toward him, slipping through the throng of people, her face unreadable as she approached.

"Well, cap cum ca," she said, her voice polite but distant as she thanked him for the evening. She didn't even look at him as she said it, her eyes scanning the exit as if she couldn't wait to leave. Mike felt a flicker of frustration rise in his chest, but he swallowed it down, forcing a smile.

"No problem," he muttered, stuffing his hands into his pockets as they made their way toward the exit. He was done with this night. The whole thing had been a disaster, and all he could think about was getting back to Soi 11, where things made sense, where he could be himself without feeling like he was being judged.

As they stepped out into the humid Bangkok night, Mike pulled out his phone, already considering texting one of the girls he knew. He needed a way to salvage the evening. Minow stood beside him, quiet for a moment, as if lost in her own thoughts. She glanced over at him, studying his face, and for a second, Mike thought she was about to say goodbye and leave him in the dust.

But then, out of nowhere, she said something that caught him completely off guard.

"I will come with you."

Mike blinked, staring at her in disbelief. He hadn't expected that. Not after the way she'd spent the entire night avoiding him, mixing with her friends while he sat alone.

"You will?" he asked, his voice a little too eager, unable to hide his surprise.

Minow nodded slowly, as if she were still trying to convince herself. She didn't smile, didn't explain why she had suddenly decided to go with him. But there was something in her eyes—an unreadable expression, somewhere between resignation and curiosity—that made Mike feel like this wasn't just a simple decision for her.

For a moment, he didn't know what to say. He had been so ready to walk away from the evening, to chalk it up as a failure and go back to the familiar comforts of his nightlife. But now, she was standing there, waiting. Waiting for him.

"Okay," he finally said, his voice steady, though his mind raced. "Let's go."

They walked in silence toward the main road, where taxis lined up waiting for the concertgoers. The tension between them was thick, but it wasn't hostile. It was more like two people standing on the edge of something unknown, unsure whether to take the leap.

As they got into the taxi, Mike couldn't shake the feeling that things had just shifted in a way he hadn't expected. He glanced at Minow, who stared out the window, her expression unreadable. He didn't know what was going to happen next, and for the first time in a long time, he felt a strange sense of excitement.

Maybe tonight hadn't been a disaster after all.

Chapter Six: One night stand

Mike woke with a start, his head pounding, the familiar dull throb of a hangover pulsing behind his eyes. The taste of stale whiskey lingered in his mouth, and for a moment, everything was a blur. He blinked, trying to make sense of his surroundings. The soft, muted light filtered through the curtains of his 39th-floor apartment, casting a warm, golden glow over the room.

He sat up slowly, the sheets tangled around his legs. His heart skipped when he glanced over at the other side of the bed. There she was—Minow. Her dark hair spilled across the pillow, her back to him, her slender frame barely covered by the sheets. He hadn't expected to see her still there, and as the fog of sleep began to clear, panic settled in.

Mike swung his legs out of the bed, his feet hitting the cold floor as he stood up. The room spun for a moment, and he had to steady himself. With a groan, he pulled open the curtains, flooding the room with blinding sunlight. Bangkok sprawled out beneath him, the city stretching endlessly into the horizon. The familiar hum of traffic, the chaotic rhythm of the streets below, brought a strange sense of normalcy to the surreal scene he found himself in.

He stood there for a moment, looking out at the city, trying to piece together the night before. The concert. The awkwardness. Minow's distance. And then—what? He remembered offering her a drink when they got back to his place. One drink had turned into several. They had sat on his balcony, talking—or trying to talk—over the noise of the city, but the details were hazy.

Had they even kissed?

He rubbed his temples, trying to remember. The harder he thought, the more elusive the memories became, like trying to hold onto water slipping through his fingers. The alcohol had done its job, blurring the edges of the night until everything felt like a dream. He turned back toward the bed, where Minow lay, and his breath caught in his throat.

She had stirred in the sunlight, raising her body slightly as the sheets slipped down, revealing her naked form. Her tattoos, dark and intricate, snaked down her back and across her ribs, patterns that looked like they told a story of their own. For a brief moment, Mike couldn't take his eyes off her. She was beautiful—there was no denying that. The kind of beauty that felt dangerous, the kind that pulled you in even when you knew better. But this wasn't the way he had wanted it. Not like this.

He closed his eyes, trying to block out the sight, hoping that when he opened them, the memory of the night before would suddenly return. But all he got were flashes—her laugh, the clink of glasses, the weight of exhaustion pulling him down as they stumbled into the apartment. He couldn't remember how she had ended up in his bed. Couldn't remember if they had... no, surely not.

A wave of dread washed over him. Had he slept with her?

The thought unsettled him in a way that was unfamiliar. It wasn't like Mike to feel guilty about things like this. He had lived years on the wild side, going from one night to the next without ever worrying about consequences. But something about Minow was different, and the idea that they might have crossed that line while he was too drunk to remember it filled him with unease.

He turned away from the window, staring at her for a moment longer. She stirred again, rolling onto her back, her eyes still closed but her face soft in the morning light. He could see the faintest lines of worry etched on her forehead, even in sleep. He wondered what she was dreaming about, if she felt the same uncertainty he did.

Mike sighed, raking a hand through his short, greying hair. He walked over to the bedside table, where the empty glasses sat, the remnants of their drinks from the night before. His wallet was still on the table, untouched. That was a relief, at least.

Suddenly, Minow stirred more fully, her eyes fluttering open, sleepy and confused. She glanced around the room for a moment before her gaze landed on Mike, standing awkwardly by the window.

"Morning," she said softly, her voice still husky from sleep.

"Uh… morning," Mike replied, shifting uncomfortably. His mind raced as he tried to figure out what to say next. He couldn't just come out and ask if they had slept together, could he?

Minow stretched, pulling the sheet up to cover herself, her face expressionless. "I didn't mean to stay," she said, almost apologetically.

Mike cleared his throat. "Yeah, uh, I don't even really remember how we got here."

She gave him a small, half-smile, but there was no humour in her eyes. "You were drunk," she said simply. "We both were."

He frowned, trying to read between the lines. "Did we… I mean, did anything happen?"

Minow stared at him for a long moment, her dark eyes unreadable. "No," she finally said, her voice quiet but firm. "You passed out as soon as you hit the bed."

Relief washed over him, though it was mixed with embarrassment. He wasn't sure what he had expected her to say, but he was thankful they hadn't crossed that line. "I'm sorry," he muttered, feeling awkward. "I didn't mean for it to—"

Minow waved a hand, cutting him off. "It's fine," she said, her tone dismissive. "We're both adults. Nothing happened, so there's no need to apologize."

Mike nodded, but the tension between them lingered, thick and uncomfortable. He watched as Minow sat up, pulling the sheet around her like a shield. She didn't seem angry, just... distant.

She glanced at the window, then back at him. "I should go."

Mike hesitated, part of him wanting to ask her to stay, another part of him relieved that she was leaving. He didn't know what to say, so he simply nodded.

Minow slipped out of bed, gathering her clothes from the floor with practiced ease. She dressed quickly, her movements smooth and deliberate, as if she had done this a hundred times before. When she was ready, she paused for a moment, looking at him with an unreadable expression.

"Thanks for the concert," she said softly, her voice flat.

"Yeah, no problem," Mike replied, feeling more and more like an outsider in his own apartment.

Without another word, Minow turned and walked out of the room, leaving Mike standing there in the harsh morning light, alone with his thoughts and the lingering feeling that, somehow, everything had just gotten more complicated.

Chapter Seven: I'm Pregnant

Mike was lounging on the balcony of his 39th-floor apartment, a cigarette in one hand, his phone in the other. It was a typical late afternoon in Bangkok, the golden light reflecting off the endless high-rises, casting long shadows across the streets below. He had just finished another night of indulgence—whiskey, clubs, girls—and was feeling the familiar combination of satisfaction and exhaustion that had become his routine.

The phone rang, and without checking the caller ID, he answered with a casual, "Yeah?"

There was a pause on the other end, and then Minow's voice came through, soft and tentative.

"Mike?"

He could tell something was off from the tone in her voice. It wasn't the usual clipped formality she used when they talked these days. He straightened up slightly, flicking ash from his cigarette over the balcony rail.

"Yeah, what's up?" he asked, his mind already drifting toward what his evening plans might be.

There was a long silence before Minow spoke again, her words hesitant, almost cautious.

"We need to talk," she began. "I have something to tell you."

Mike's brow furrowed, a flicker of concern passing through him. He took another drag of his cigarette, forcing himself to stay calm. "Alright. What is it?"

Minow hesitated again, and when she finally spoke, the words came out in a rush, as if she had been holding them back for too long.

"I'm pregnant."

Mike froze, the cigarette halfway to his lips. He blinked, processing her words but not fully registering them. Pregnant. The word hung in the air between them, heavy and undeniable.

"We're going to have a Luke clung baby," Minow added quietly. Her voice was soft but steady, almost resigned.

Mike's mind reeled, the world around him narrowing down to the phone in his hand. A Luke clung baby—a mixed-race baby. His baby. He hadn't thought about children, not seriously. At 46, he had accepted that kids weren't going to be part of his life. He hadn't wanted them. He had enjoyed his freedom too much, his nights in the clubs, his indulgent lifestyle.

But now, hearing Minow's words, something shifted inside him. He felt... excited. Unexpectedly, irrationally excited.

"Are you sure?" he asked, his voice unsteady, barely above a whisper.

"Yes," Minow replied. "I'm sure. I went to the doctor today. It's real, Mike. We're going to have a baby."

Mike felt a strange sensation ripple through him, a mixture of fear and exhilaration. A baby. His baby. He had spent years building a life for himself that revolved around nothing but indulgence—no commitments, no responsibilities. Yet the idea of having a child, something he had never wanted, suddenly ignited something deep inside him.

"Well, shit," he said, running a hand through his hair. A grin spread across his face, unexpected and uncontrollable. "That's... that's amazing."

On the other end of the line, Minow let out a small, breathy laugh. "You're not angry?"

"Angry?" Mike repeated, still grinning. "No. I mean, I wasn't planning on it, but hell, I'm 46. It's probably about time, right?"

Minow didn't respond immediately. He could hear her breathing, as if she were waiting for something else, something more serious.

"So, what now?" Mike asked, still on that strange high of sudden excitement.

"Well," Minow began, "I'll need to move back in. I'll need help, Mike. And you need to start thinking about this... about us." Her voice was calm, but there was a quiet urgency behind her words.

Mike leaned back in his chair, taking another drag of his cigarette. "Yeah, yeah," he muttered, waving his hand as if she could see it. "You can move back in. We'll figure it out."

His mind was already moving on, thinking about how this new situation could fit into his life. He wasn't going to give up his freedom—not entirely. He liked his nights, his girls, his whiskey. Minow moving in wasn't going to change that. She'd just be there, like a wife. She could cook, clean, take care of the apartment while he carried on with his life. The baby? That would come later. He'd deal with it when it arrived.

"Are you okay with this?" Minow asked after a pause, her voice soft and careful, as though she wasn't sure how to gauge his reaction.

Mike smiled, even though she couldn't see it. "Yeah, Minow. I'm more than okay."

They hung up soon after, and Mike remained on the balcony, staring out over the city as the sun began to sink behind the skyline. The thought of fatherhood, which should have terrified him, instead thrilled him in a way he hadn't expected. He'd never considered himself the fatherly type, but maybe that was about to change.

The next few weeks went by in a blur. Minow moved back into the apartment, slipping into the role of housekeeper and cook with quiet efficiency. She was still distant, but she kept the place clean, made his meals, and even started to prepare baby things. It was almost like having a wife, but without any of the emotional connection. Mike liked it that way. It was comfortable, easy.

And while Minow began to settle into her new role, Mike's life barely changed. He still spent his nights in the clubs, drinking with friends, surrounded by girls from Soi 11. He still paid bar fines, still lost himself in the chaos of the city's nightlife. The only difference was that now, when he came home late at night, Minow was there, sleeping in the apartment, waiting for him.

Sometimes, she would wake up when he stumbled in, her eyes following him as he drunkenly made his way to bed. But she never said anything. She never asked where he had been or who he had been with. Mike assumed she knew—how could she not?—but she never brought it up.

And that suited him just fine. He wasn't going to change. The baby might be coming, but for now, life carried on as usual.

Mike stood on the balcony one night, staring out over the city again, his cigarette glowing in the dark. He could hear Minow moving around inside, tidying up after dinner. A smile tugged at the corner of his mouth.

A Luke clung baby.

The idea still thrilled him, but it hadn't hit him yet—not really. It was still abstract, something in the future, something that wouldn't change his world too much. For now, everything was just the way he liked it. And as far as Mike was concerned, that was all that mattered.

Chapter Eight: Year one

The year that followed was a whirlwind for Mike and Minow, a blur of unexpected milestones that neither had fully anticipated. Just twelve months after their first awkward meeting in a bar on Soi 11, everything had changed. They were now married, parents, and on their way to England, leaving the chaotic, neon-lit nights of Bangkok behind.

Mike stood in the maternity ward, staring through the glass at the rows of newborns. His son, their son, lay swaddled in a tiny blue blanket, his eyes barely open. Itsada. Minow had chosen the name, telling Mike that it meant "supreme power" in Thai. Mike liked the sound of it—strong, masculine, just like he wanted his boy to be.

The birth had been quick, faster than Mike had expected. He hadn't been by Minow's side for much of it. Hospitals made him uncomfortable, so he'd spent most of the time pacing in the hallway, checking his phone, and texting a few friends to let them know the news. When the nurse finally told him the baby had arrived, he'd stepped in for a few minutes, looked at the small, squirming bundle in Minow's arms, muttered a half-hearted "Congratulations," and then, as quickly as he had come, he left.

He told himself it wasn't a big deal. He wasn't cut out for the whole dad thing—not yet, at least. And besides, there were other things on his mind. After all, Bangkok's nightlife didn't sleep just because he had a newborn.

Minutes after Itsada was born, Mike was back on Soi 11, celebrating his son's arrival in the only way he knew how: surrounded by girls, alcohol, and the familiar buzz of the city. The same bar where he had first met Minow now felt like the only place he could relax, where life still made sense to him. Minow knew where he was, of course. She hadn't asked, hadn't pleaded for him to stay by her side. That wasn't their dynamic. She had her role, and he had his.

The weeks after the birth passed in a blur, much like the rest of their relationship. A rushed, impersonal wedding ceremony at a registry office had taken place just weeks before Itsada's birth, mostly for convenience. They'd exchanged rings, signed the papers, and left without fanfare. The reception? A quick stop at The Pickled

Liver, a British pub on Soi 11, where Mike and Minow had sat at the bar together, nursing drinks in silence. It wasn't the kind of celebration most couples would have, but it was enough for them.

Minow had left early that night, exhausted from the pregnancy and the weight of the future pressing down on her. She had kissed Mike on the cheek, thanked him, and returned to the apartment. Mike, on the other hand, stayed behind, drinking well into the night with the same girls he had always spent his time with. It wasn't about betrayal—there was nothing emotional between him and the girls. It was just habit, a way to keep the loneliness at bay.

But Whoredom, as Mike had come to call it, had lost some of its allure. The life he had once relished—night after night in clubs, surrounded by strangers and fleeting pleasures—was starting to feel hollow. Itsada's birth had awakened something in him, something unfamiliar. It wasn't exactly love, but there was a strange pull now, a sense that maybe it was time to leave that part of his life behind. Besides, Bangkok's streets weren't as welcoming as they once had been. He could feel it in the way the city looked at him, like he no longer belonged.

And so, Mike didn't mind leaving. The move to England had come as a surprise, even to him. After Itsada's birth, Minow had been desperate for stability, for something more than the transient life they had built in Bangkok. Mike worked in the Middle East, flying in and out for 28-day stints, and Minow was left alone in an apartment that had once been her cage. She wanted more for her son, more than Bangkok's chaotic streets and fleeting glances could offer.

When Mike suggested England, she agreed without hesitation. It was a chance to start over, to give Itsada something solid. And so, a few months after the baby was born, they packed their lives into a few suitcases and boarded the flight.

The small house in England felt worlds away from the life Mike had known. It was quiet, too quiet at times, with the hum of the

English countryside replacing the chaotic buzz of Bangkok. Mike had grown up here, in this sleepy town, but it no longer felt like home. He didn't mind though; he wasn't planning on spending much time here. His job in the Middle East kept him away for most of the year. Every 28 days, he would return, spend a few weeks with Minow and Itsada, and then pack up and leave again.

It was an arrangement that worked for him. Minow handled the house, took care of the baby, and made sure everything ran smoothly while he was gone. It was a strange kind of domesticity, but it suited Mike just fine. He wasn't cut out for the day-to-day of fatherhood, and besides, the thought of being tied down still made his skin crawl.

Minow, for her part, adapted quickly to life in England, though Mike knew it wasn't easy for her. She was far from home, far from the HiSo crowd she had once known, and now living in a small, quiet town where she knew no one. Her days were spent caring for their son, cooking, cleaning, and doing all the things she had once avoided. It wasn't glamorous, but she had Itsada, and that was enough for her—for now.

Mike's returns were always the same. He'd come back from the Middle East, tired but restless, and for a few days, he'd play the part of a family man. He'd hold Itsada awkwardly, smile at Minow, and pretend that this was the life he had always wanted. But the truth was, it was all just a waiting game. He was already counting down the days until he could leave again, until he could return to the freedom he found in the Middle East, where he wasn't tethered to the expectations of fatherhood and marriage.

On Itsada's first birthday, Mike was home, but barely present. He had flown in the night before, exhausted from the trip, and had only spent a few minutes with his son before retreating to bed. The next morning, Minow had prepared a small cake, just the three of them in their quiet house. Itsada was oblivious to the occasion, babbling happily in his highchair as Minow lit the single candle on the cake.

Mike watched, feeling distant, detached. He loved his son—or at least, he thought he did—but the weight of responsibility felt suffocating. As soon as Minow blew out the candle for Itsada, Mike made an excuse, kissed his wife on the cheek, and slipped out of the house.

That night, he found a bar in town—nothing like the ones on Soi 11, but it would do. He sat alone, nursing a drink, thinking about Bangkok, about the life he had left behind, and wondering if he had made the right choice.

Chapter Nine: Spare room

The shift was gradual, but unmistakable. By the time Mike moved into the spare room, it felt inevitable, like something that had been building for months, maybe even years, ever since the day they landed in England. The excitement that had once coursed through him when Minow had first told him she was

pregnant had long faded. In its place was a
dull, numbing routine. His days were spent
either working in the Middle East or killing
time in the house before he could leave
again.

The spare room was small, barely big
enough for a single bed and a wardrobe, but
it suited him fine. The distance between him
and Minow had grown so wide that sharing
a bed seemed pointless, even painful. He
couldn't remember the last time they had
touched, the last time they had even really
spoken. It wasn't as though he disliked
her—there was no outright animosity
between them—but there was nothing left to
say.

Every night, he could hear her through the
thin walls. The muffled sound of her crying
drifted from the master bedroom, where she
now slept alone in the big double bed they
had once shared. It was a sound that gnawed
at him, but he pushed it aside, told himself it
wasn't his problem. After all, it wasn't him

she was crying for. It was home—Thailand. The country she missed with every fibre of her being. Her friends, the food, the bustling streets of Bangkok.

Here, in this cold, grey English town, Minow was a stranger. Isolated, alone, trapped in a place where the sun rarely shone, and the food was bland and foreign to her. She had tried, in the beginning, to adapt. She cooked Thai food when she could, but the ingredients here weren't the same. The spices were dull, the herbs impossible to find. Even when she did manage to recreate a dish, it didn't taste right. Nothing felt right.

Mike would see her in the kitchen sometimes, standing over the oven with a look of quiet determination on her face, trying to make something that would remind her of home. But the sadness never left her eyes, not really.

Her only solace was their son, Itsada. He was the one thing that tethered her to this life, the one source of joy in a place that otherwise felt suffocating. She loved him fiercely, more than anything. She would spend hours playing with him, holding him, teaching him the few Thai words she could manage to slip in between the English he was rapidly learning. But even that love, deep as it was, couldn't fill the hole that had opened inside her since leaving Thailand.

Mike could feel the distance between them growing wider every day, but he couldn't bring himself to do anything about it. He had his own frustrations, his own regrets. He knew, deep down, that he had dragged her into this life, into this country, without ever really asking if it was what she wanted. They had moved so fast—marriage, the baby, the move—and now they were paying the price.

He lay awake most nights, staring at the ceiling, listening to the sounds of Minow's sobs. Part of him felt guilty, but another part of him was simply tired. Tired of the weight of their relationship, tired of the responsibility that came with being a husband and father.

Sometimes, when he was in the Middle East, he would think about the life he had left behind in Bangkok. The freedom, the ease of it all. The clubs, the girls, the drinks. It had been a hollow life, sure, but it had been his life. Now, he felt trapped in a house that wasn't a home, with a woman he barely knew anymore.

He wondered if Minow felt the same way. She had never said it out loud, but he could see it in her eyes. The way she looked out of the window at the grey skies, as though searching for something she knew she'd never find here. The way her face would light up for a moment when she heard Thai spoken on the rare occasion, only for the light to fade when the moment passed.

The nights were the worst. Alone in her big bed, Minow would cry herself to sleep. She wasn't crying for Mike—that much was clear. She was crying for the life she had left behind, for the person she had once been. Back in Bangkok, she had been someone, surrounded by friends, immersed in a culture she understood, a world she belonged to.

Here, in this cold, foreign place, she felt invisible.

Mike could hear her crying, but he never went to her. What would he even say? He couldn't fix this for her. He couldn't bring Thailand to her doorstep, couldn't give her back the life she had lost.

In the mornings, they barely spoke. Mike would shuffle out of the spare room, still groggy, and find Minow already awake, feeding Itsada or cleaning up after breakfast. She was efficient, going about her duties with a quiet sense of purpose, but there was no joy in it. She never smiled anymore. At least, not at him.

Itsada was the only one who could make her smile. When he giggled or reached out for her, her face would soften, her eyes brightening for a brief moment. But even that smile was tinged with sadness, as though she knew that no matter how much she loved her son, it wasn't enough to fill the emptiness inside her.

Mike knew that this situation couldn't last forever. Something had to give. But for now, they were both just existing, going through the motions of a life neither of them had really chosen. He would continue his rotations to the Middle East, come home for a few weeks, then leave again, while Minow stayed behind, alone in the house, alone with their son.

It wasn't the life either of them had envisioned when they had first met. But it was the life they had now, and neither of them seemed to know how to change it. Minow longed for Thailand, and Mike longed for something he couldn't quite define. They were both trapped in a place they didn't want to be, bound together by a son they both loved but who couldn't fix what was broken between them.

And so, every night, Mike would lie in his narrow bed, listening to Minow's soft cries from the room next door, knowing that neither of them had the courage to face the truth: that maybe, just maybe, this wasn't enough anymore. For either of them.

Chapter Ten: Self Harm

The house had grown colder in more ways than one. As the seasons shifted, the grey skies of the English town only seemed to mirror the darkness creeping into Minow's mind. Her days blurred together—each one as bleak as the last. There were no friends, no familiar faces, no food that brought her comfort. Just the overwhelming silence of a place that wasn't hers and the crushing weight of her own isolation.

It started slowly at first. Mike noticed small things—Minow withdrawing further, spending more time alone, her voice quieter when she spoke, if she spoke at all. The distance between them had grown so vast that it was hard for Mike to recognize the woman he'd once been so captivated by. Her once radiant smile, the sparkle in her eyes, had long since vanished, replaced by a blankness that unnerved him.

Then came the cuts.

At first, they were small. Tiny slashes on her arms, barely noticeable unless you were looking for them. Mike had found them by accident one evening when she was washing the dishes. He'd reached for a cup and noticed the faint red marks, crisscrossing her wrists like spiderwebs. He didn't say anything at first, unsure of what he had seen. Maybe it was nothing—maybe she had just been careless in the kitchen.

But it wasn't nothing. The cuts grew deeper, more frequent. She began wearing long sleeves, even in the heat of the house, to hide them. Mike had caught glimpses of her arms when she rolled up her sleeves while bathing Itsada, the sight of the angry red lines jolting him every time. He knew what it was, but he didn't know how to address it. He wasn't good at talking about feelings—never had been. And Minow wasn't the type to open up, not even to him.

Then came the knives.

Mike found her in the kitchen one evening, her back to him as she stood at the counter, her hand gripping the handle of a large kitchen knife. She was perfectly still, the blade held in front of her, pointed toward her own skin. He froze, his breath catching in his throat as the reality of the situation hit him. This was no longer just about small cuts—this was something far darker, far more dangerous.

"Minow," he said softly, stepping forward slowly, as if approaching a wild animal.

She didn't respond, didn't even turn to look at him. Her eyes were fixed on the knife, her breathing slow and shallow.

"Put it down," Mike urged, his voice trembling, unsure of what to do. His heart pounded in his chest as he closed the distance between them, his hands outstretched, ready to grab the blade if he had to.

Minow didn't move, her grip tightening around the knife. Tears silently streamed down her face, her body shaking with sobs she tried to suppress.

In that moment, something in Mike snapped. The fear of losing her, the fear of seeing her blood on the floor, overrode everything else. He lunged forward, grabbing her wrist, twisting the knife out of her hand. She fought him, screaming, the anguish spilling out of her in a way he had never seen before.

"Let go!" she cried, her voice hoarse, almost primal, as she struggled against him.

Mike held on, his arms shaking as he wrestled the knife away from her. She wasn't strong, but the sheer force of her desperation made the struggle terrifying. In the chaos, he pinned her against the wall, his hand around her throat, not to hurt her, but to hold her still. His other hand pried the knife from her grip, tossing it to the floor with a loud clatter.

For a moment, everything was silent. Minow stopped struggling, her body slumping against the wall, exhausted from the fight. Mike stood there, panting, his hand still around her neck, his own pulse racing. His mind raced, trying to process what had just happened.

And then, the sound that shattered everything:

"Daddy?"

Mike's head snapped around, his eyes locking onto Itsada, who stood in the doorway, wide-eyed, clutching his small stuffed elephant. The boy had seen everything—the fight, the knife, his father holding his mother by the throat. He was too young to understand, but old enough to know something was terribly wrong.

"Go to your room, Itsada," Mike said, his voice strained, but the boy didn't move. He just stood there, frozen in place, staring at his parents with a look that Mike would never forget.

That moment would haunt them all.

Mike released his grip on Minow, his hands shaking as he stepped back. She slid down the wall, her body crumpling to the floor as she sobbed uncontrollably. Mike, still in shock, turned to Itsada, unsure of what to say, unsure of how to explain what had just happened.

The days that followed were a blur. Mike did his best to remove anything sharp from the house—knives, scissors, razors. He even risked injury to himself in the process, one night slicing his hand open while hurriedly trying to hide the last kitchen knife in a cupboard. He had no idea if it would make a difference, but it was all he could think to do.

Minow's depression deepened after that. She barely spoke, barely moved. She spent most of her time in bed, the heavy weight of despair dragging her down. Mike knew she was spiralling, but he didn't know how to help her. He was terrified of another incident, terrified that the next time she picked up a knife, he wouldn't be there in time to stop her.

Meanwhile, Itsada, who had always been a joyful, bright child, seemed to change overnight. He stopped laughing as much, stopped playing with his toys. He would watch his parents with wary eyes, as if waiting for the next explosion. The sight of Mike and Minow fighting—Mike pinning his mother to the wall—had left a mark on him, a mark that neither of them could erase.

One evening, as Mike sat alone in the living room, his hands shaking from the stress of it all, Itsada climbed onto his lap. The boy didn't say anything at first. He just sat there, silent, his small hand resting on Mike's arm.

"Daddy," Itsada whispered, his voice barely audible. "Is Mommy going to be okay?"

Mike's heart broke in that moment. He had no answer for his son. He didn't know if Minow would ever be okay again. He didn't know how to fix what was broken in their family, didn't know if he even could.

"I hope so, buddy," Mike finally said, his voice cracking. "I hope so."

But deep down, he wasn't sure if hope was enough.

Chapter Eleven: Paranoia.

The years that followed the harrowing incident in the kitchen saw the family settle into an uneasy routine, a delicate balance that could be tipped at any moment. Minow's struggles never entirely disappeared, but the frequency of the worst episodes diminished, replaced by a sort of numb acceptance of her new life. The house remained cold and quiet most of the time, but there were periods of stability—moments when Mike dared to hope that they might have reached a fragile peace.

Every few months, Minow would take a flight back to Thailand, leaving Mike and Itsada behind. Those trips became her lifeline. The anticipation of returning home was the only thing that brought a flicker of light back into her eyes. It was a chance to reconnect with friends, to eat the food she craved, to be surrounded by the familiar sights and sounds of her homeland. Mike would watch her as she packed, a different woman emerging from the shell she wore in England. She'd hum softly to herself, eyes alight with the excitement of leaving.

For Mike, those trips were a relief too. He'd get to spend time alone with Itsada, just the two of them. He cherished that month when Minow was gone—no arguments, no awkward silences. He would take his son to football practice, cook simple meals, and try to provide some semblance of normalcy for the boy. Itsada thrived in those periods, the tension in the house lifting like a fog clearing from a field.

But whenever Minow returned, the atmosphere would shift again. She'd walk through the door, the scent of Thailand still clinging to her clothes, and it was as if she were a stranger all over again. The joy that had carried her through her time abroad faded almost immediately, replaced by the same hollow expression she wore day in and day out in England.

It became a cycle they all grew accustomed to—until the last trip.

When Minow returned that time, she was different. Something had happened, something Mike couldn't quite place at first. She came through the door gaunt and pale, her once-sparkling eyes dulled with a new kind of fear. She'd lost weight—too much weight—and her hands trembled as she fumbled with her bags. She didn't greet Itsada with her usual tight embrace, didn't immediately start chattering about the things she'd seen and done. Instead, she stood there in the entryway, her gaze darting around the house as if expecting someone to leap out of the shadows.

"Minow, what's wrong?" Mike asked, concern rising in his chest. He stepped toward her, but she recoiled, backing away as if afraid he'd touch her.

"They're coming," she whispered, her voice a hushed rasp. "They're coming for me. I... I made a mistake, Mike."

It took days for him to get the full story out of her. At first, her words were disjointed, almost nonsensical. She mumbled to herself, eyes darting around the room, muttering about "powerful people" and "the King" in a way that made Mike's skin crawl. He'd heard her talk like this before, back when the depression had been at its peak, but this was different. There was a frantic edge to her paranoia, a terror he'd never seen in her before.

"Minow, calm down. Who's coming? What happened?" He tried to keep his voice gentle, but panic was clawing at his throat. He needed her to make sense, needed to understand what had happened to her in Thailand.

Finally, after several days of coaxing and pleading, she told him everything. She had been at a party with some of her old HiSo friends, the kind of lavish gathering she used to frequent back when her life had been so different. It had felt good, she said, to be surrounded by luxury again, to feel like she belonged somewhere. But things had taken a dark turn. There had been drinks, more than she should have had, and then someone had offered her something else—a little white pill that promised to take the night to the next level.

"I didn't want to take it, Mike," she whimpered, staring down at her shaking hands. "I swear, I didn't. But they—they pressured me. They said it would be fun."

The rest of the night was a blur in her memory, fragments of bright lights and laughter swirling in a haze. She remembered dancing, felt the music thumping through her veins, remembered someone—she couldn't say who—guiding her to a back room. There had been more people there, some she recognized, others she didn't. And then... the incident.

"I don't know what I said, Mike. I don't even remember." Her voice cracked as she spoke, her fingers clutching at the hem of her shirt. "But they showed me the video. They showed me what I did."

Apparently, at some point during the night, she had said something—something that could be construed as disrespectful toward the King of Thailand. In her inebriated state, she had made a gesture, a joke, something innocuous to her foggy mind but damning in the eyes of others. Someone had filmed it, and the video had been shared online.

"They're going to kill me," she whispered, her face pale and drawn. "Powerful people, Mike. People who know the Red Bull family, people who control things in Thailand. They're coming. They know where I am."

Mike didn't know what to say. He stared at her, the disbelief and fear warring within him. It sounded insane, but he could see the desperation in her eyes. She believed it— every word of it. Minow had become convinced that she was being hunted, that men would show up at their door any day now to make her pay for a mistake she didn't even remember making.

He tried to reason with her, tried to get her to see a doctor, but she refused. She started refusing everything—doctor's appointments, phone calls from her friends, even her own family back in Thailand. She changed the passwords on her internet banking and withdrew what little savings she had, convinced that someone was hacking into her accounts. She wouldn't sleep alone, instead squeezing into Mike's single bed, clutching his arm with a vice-like grip as she muttered about men in black, about the "Thai Ninjas" who were going to come for her.

"I need you to believe me, Mike," she begged one night, her voice trembling. "They're going to kill me. You don't understand how powerful they are. The man from Red Bull—he's behind this. They're watching everything I do."

Mike felt a wave of helplessness wash over him as he listened to her. He didn't know what to believe. He wanted to tell her that it was all in her head, that no one was coming to hurt her. But he couldn't reach her. The fear had dug too deep, consumed too much of her. She jumped at every sound, flinched whenever the phone rang. Even the sight of an unfamiliar car passing by the house would send her into a fit of panic.

Minow's paranoia was tearing their family apart, and there was nothing he could do to stop it. Itsada, now older and more aware, would look at his mother with wide, frightened eyes, confusion and worry etched on his small face.

"Mom are we safe?" he asked one day, his voice small and scared.

"Yes, sweetheart," Minow said, forcing a smile that didn't reach her eyes. "We're safe. I won't let them hurt us."

But even as she said it, Mike knew she didn't believe it. And that was the worst part of all.

Chapter Twelve: Third time 'unlucky'

The door creaked open slowly, and Mike squinted against the light flooding in from the hallway. It was the middle of the night, and he was groggy, the remnants of sleep clinging stubbornly to his senses. But something in the way Minow hovered in the doorway snapped him fully awake.

"Mike...," she whispered, her voice carrying a strange, hollow quality that sent a shiver down his spine.

He sat up, his eyes adjusting to the dim glow of the bedside lamp. She stepped into the room, her movements slow and deliberate. That's when he saw it—the small, trembling hand outstretched toward him, a pile of colourful pills resting precariously on her palm. There were at least twenty of them, a lethal rainbow of sedatives, painkillers, and who knew what else.

"What are you doing, Minow?" His voice was low, but he could hear the strain in it, the anger and fear threatening to choke him.

She looked at him, her gaze flat and unblinking. And then, without a word, she opened her mouth and lifted the pills toward it.

"Minow! Stop!" Mike lunged forward, grabbing her wrist just as she tried to shove the handful of tablets down her throat. He twisted her arm away from her face, the pills scattering across the floor like tiny beads. She didn't fight him; she just stood there, limp and defeated, as if he'd stolen the last bit of strength she had left.

"I want to die, Mike," she whispered, her voice breaking. "I can't take it anymore. They're going to kill me anyway. I just want it to end before they do it."

Mike held her wrist tightly, his knuckles white. He could feel the delicate bones beneath her skin, feel the way her pulse fluttered frantically beneath his grip. He forced himself to loosen his hold, his eyes narrowing as he looked up at her.

"Don't be ridiculous, Minow," he said, his voice hard. "This—this is just stupid. You're not going to die. You're not even trying to kill yourself; you're just doing this for attention."

Minow flinched as if he'd struck her. She took a step back, her face crumpling. "No, Mike. You don't understand. You've never understood."

"Understand what?" he snapped, throwing his hands up in exasperation. "Understand that you want to leave your son without a mother? Understand that you want to abandon him because of some made-up fear? Grow up, Minow."

Tears welled in her eyes, but she quickly turned away, hurrying out of the room without another word. Mike stared after her, his heart still pounding. He listened as she walked down the hall, the sound of her footsteps fading away. A few minutes later, he heard her bedroom door click shut, and the house was silent once more.

That was the first time. But it wasn't the last.

A few days later, Mike came home to find Minow hunched over the kitchen sink, her face pale and slick with sweat. An empty bottle of bleach sat on the counter beside her, the cap discarded and rolling back and forth on the tiles.

"Minow, what the hell—?" He strode over, yanking the bottle out of her reach. She looked up at him, her eyes wide and glassy.

"I drank it, Mike," she whispered, her voice raw and strained. "I drank it because I want to die. I want to die so bad."

For a second, he thought he saw a flash of triumph in her eyes, as if she'd finally found a way to make him see how desperate she was. But then her face twisted, and she doubled over, retching violently into the sink. The acrid stench of the cleaning fluid filled the air, mingling with the sour smell of bile. He watched her heave and gag, her body convulsing with each painful spasm.

Disgust and anger warred within him. He should have called an ambulance. He should have taken her to the hospital. But instead, he stood there, gripping the empty bottle and watching her suffer.

"Stop it, Minow," he muttered, his voice cold. "Just stop this. You're not dying. You're just making yourself sick. This is pathetic."

She looked up at him, her eyes bloodshot and streaming with tears. "You don't care, do you? You really don't care if I die."

"No, I don't," he shot back, the words coming out sharper than he intended. "If you really wanted to die, you wouldn't keep doing this where I can see you. You'd go off somewhere and actually do it. But you won't, will you?"

Minow stared at him for a long moment, something breaking in her gaze. Then she turned back to the sink, coughing weakly, her body slumping in defeat. He didn't reach out to comfort her. He didn't touch her at all. He just turned and walked out of the kitchen, leaving her alone.

The third time, it was almost comical.

Mike had been watching TV when the front door burst open. Minow stumbled in, dripping wet and shivering, her clothes soaked through. Her hair hung in limp strands around her face, and water pooled around her feet, spreading in a growing puddle across the carpet.

"What now?" he sighed, not even bothering to get up.

"I jumped," she said, her teeth chattering violently. "I jumped in the river."

He raised an eyebrow, his gaze flicking over her sodden form. "And you're standing here telling me this because…?"

"Because I couldn't drown." Her voice was high and shaky, on the edge of hysteria. "I tried, Mike. I really tried. But this stupid jacket—it kept me afloat. I couldn't sink. I couldn't die."

She gestured to the puffer jacket she was wearing, the thick material puffed up like a life vest. It was ridiculous, really—this tiny, fragile woman standing there, soaked to the bone and furious at her own survival because of a piece of clothing.

Mike shook his head, a bitter laugh escaping his lips. "So, what? You want me to feel sorry for you? You want me to take pity on you because you failed at killing yourself again?"

Minow's face crumpled, and she let out a sob, her shoulders shaking. "They're coming, Mike. The Thai Ninjas… they're coming for me. I just want it to be over before they get here. I don't want to live like this anymore."

He stood up then, walking over to her. For a moment, he just looked at her—this woman he'd once thought was the most beautiful creature he'd ever seen. Now she was a shadow, a wraith, consumed by her own fear and madness.

"Minow," he said quietly, "no one is coming for you. You're doing this to yourself. And I can't help you. I can't save you. I don't even know if I want to try anymore."

With that, he turned and walked away, leaving her standing there in the doorway, dripping and broken.

In the weeks that followed, he hid every sharp object in the house, threw out every bottle of cleaning fluid. He knew it wouldn't stop her if she was truly determined, but he couldn't watch her self-destruct right in front of him again. Not like that.

But the fear, the paranoia—it didn't leave her. It only grew, eating away at what little was left of her sanity. And Mike found himself withdrawing further and further, unable to face the horror of what his life had become.

Every night, he lay awake in his small, cramped bed, listening to Minow's quiet sobs drifting through the walls. He could hear the soft murmurs of her voice as she whispered to herself, pleading with invisible enemies to spare her. And every morning, he would rise, a little more numb, a little more broken, and go about his day as if nothing had changed.

But everything had changed. And there was no going back.

Chapter Thirteen: Turning point

For months, the household had moved like clockwork through its dreary routine, each day blending seamlessly into the next. Minow stayed hidden in her bedroom, shrouded in shadows and silence. The blinds were always drawn, and the room smelled stale, like fear had soaked into the very walls. She rarely emerged except to shuffle to the kitchen, eyes darting anxiously around as if expecting to see her imagined pursuers lurking in the corners.

But then, one day, something shifted.

It started with a phone call. Mike had come home to find Minow sitting at the kitchen table, her hair tangled and her face drawn, clutching her mobile phone like it was a lifeline. Her knuckles were white, her lips pursed, and there was something almost fragile in the way she held herself, as if she might shatter at the slightest touch.

"I... I talked to him," she whispered when Mike asked what was going on. "The man. The one who said he was with Red Bull."

Mike's heart sank. He felt his patience thinning, the familiar exasperation bubbling up again. Here we go, he thought, steeling himself for another incoherent rant.

But then Minow looked up at him, her eyes clearer than he'd seen them in months.

"He's not real, Mike," she said, her voice trembling. "He never was. I... I found out. He's just some scammer pretending to be someone important. He doesn't own Red Bull. He has no power. None of it was true."

Mike stared at her, trying to process what she was saying. "What do you mean?"

"He doesn't know anyone," she continued, shaking her head slowly. "No one's coming to kill me. The social media thing—it's all died down. I'm… I'm not in danger."

He blinked, still not quite believing what he was hearing. "So… you're saying you were wrong?"

"Yes," Minow whispered, her voice cracking. "I was wrong. I… I'm sorry, Mike. I was so scared. I just—"

Mike's shoulders sagged as a weight he hadn't even realized he was carrying seemed to lift ever so slightly. He exhaled, not quite sure what to say. Relief washed over him, mingled with the remnants of anger and frustration, but most of all, a cautious hope.

"Does this mean… you're okay now?" he asked carefully, not daring to be too optimistic.

She nodded, a small, hesitant smile forming on her lips. "I think so. I want to try, Mike. I want to be… normal again."

Those words—simple, almost ordinary—hit Mike harder than he could have imagined. He didn't respond, just nodded stiffly, unsure how to react. He'd heard promises like this before, seen flickers of hope flare up only to be extinguished again. But something in Minow's gaze told him this was different. There was a determination there, a strength he hadn't seen in a long time.

In the days that followed, small but noticeable changes began to occur.

Minow got out of bed. She washed her hair. She changed into clean clothes. It was slow, painfully so at times, but she was making an effort. Little by little, she started to come back to life.

Mike tried to stay out of her way, not wanting to disrupt whatever fragile progress she was making. He kept his distance, hovering in the background like a wary spectator. He watched her from afar as she tentatively ventured outside to the garden, her movements tentative, as if relearning how to walk in the daylight.

And then, one morning, she did something he hadn't seen her do in what felt like forever—she showered.

He was passing by the bathroom when he heard the water running, the sound startling him. He hesitated outside the door, listening. The shower curtain rustled softly, and he caught a glimpse of her silhouette through the frosted glass—slender, graceful, and unmistakably familiar.

Mike knew he should walk away. He should give her privacy; respect the space she was carving out for herself. But something kept him rooted to the spot, his gaze drawn almost against his will.

The water cascaded down her body, slicking her long black hair to her back, glistening on her smooth skin. She moved slowly, turning to let the water wash over her face, her hands running up and down her arms as if she were scrubbing away the last remnants of fear and paranoia that had clung to her like a second skin.

Mike swallowed; his throat suddenly dry. He knew he shouldn't be looking, shouldn't be feeling what he was feeling. But there was something almost mesmerizing about the sight of her, something raw and vulnerable that stirred emotions he'd thought long dead.

Minow raised her arms, rinsing out her hair, and as she turned, the curve of her body caught the light. The old tattoos on her skin, faded but still distinct, told the story of a different time—a different Minow. He felt a strange, unexpected pang of… what? Desire? Longing?

He hadn't thought of her like that in years. Their marriage had become a cold, mechanical arrangement, a shared burden rather than a relationship. And yet, here he was, feeling something, he couldn't quite name, watching her through the thin veil of steam.

She had no idea he was there. He should leave—he knew that. But he couldn't tear his eyes away. He stood there, his pulse quickening, until the sound of the water turning off snapped him back to reality.

He turned and walked away quickly, his heart thumping uncomfortably in his chest.

Minow's return to the world was tentative at first. She started by going to the local grocery store, then ventured further, taking longer walks around the neighbourhood. The first time she came back with a shopping bag full of fresh vegetables and spices, she looked almost... pleased with herself.

"I thought I'd make us a proper Thai dinner," she announced shyly, glancing at Mike.

He nodded, keeping his expression neutral. "That sounds good."

And it was good. The food tasted almost like the dishes she used to make back in Bangkok, filled with the vibrant flavours he'd nearly forgotten. It was the first time they'd eaten together at the dining table in months.

Slowly, Minow began to rebuild a routine. She'd wake up early, get dressed, and even help Itsada with his schoolwork. There were setbacks, of course—days when the paranoia seemed to creep back in, when she'd spend hours checking and re-checking her phone for messages that never came. But overall, she was getting better.

Mike didn't say much, but he noticed everything. He watched her with a guarded sort of hope, afraid to believe that this might be the beginning of something new. He couldn't let himself get too comfortable. He'd seen how quickly she could spiral.

But for now, things were… better. The house didn't feel quite as suffocating, the air not quite as thick with tension. There was laughter sometimes, small bursts of it when Minow played with Itsada or teased Mike about his terrible cooking.

One evening, as he stood in the doorway of the kitchen, watching Minow stir a pot of

Tom Yum soup, he felt a strange sense of peace settle over him. She glanced up and caught his eye, smiling softly.

"Thank you," she murmured.

"For what?"

"For not giving up on me," she said simply.

Mike didn't know how to respond. He wasn't sure he deserved her gratitude, not after all the things he'd said and done. But he nodded, swallowing down the lump in his throat.

"Just… keep getting better, okay?" he managed to say.

Minow nodded, her smile widening. "I will, Mike. I promise."

It was a fragile promise, one that could shatter at any moment. But it was enough—for now.

Chapter Fourteen: The Past

Mike noticed the change slowly at first. It was subtle—small shifts in the way Minow spoke, her gaze drifting off more frequently, a hint of something faraway in her eyes. She'd always had a tendency to reminisce about her life back in Thailand, but lately, it was different. Every conversation, every memory she shared, seemed to focus obsessively on her childhood.

"When I was a little girl," she'd start almost every sentence, her voice soft, eyes wide as if she were actually back there, reliving it all. "I helped my mum in the bakery, you know. We used to wake up at three in the morning, kneading the dough and shaping the pastries. My hands were so small back then—too small to lift the heavy bags of flour."

She'd go on, describing the scent of pandan leaves and coconut milk filling the air, the early morning mist rolling off the canal beside their house, the neighbours calling out greetings as they passed by on their way to the market. Mike would sit there, half-listening, nodding occasionally. But as the days wore on, her stories grew more intense, more vivid.

"It's like I was cursed, Mike. Bad luck followed me everywhere, even when I was a child," she muttered one evening, her eyes distant. "My father left us when I was only six. He just walked away, left me and Mum alone. I tried so hard to be a good girl, to help. But it didn't matter. I always felt... empty. Like there was something wrong with me."

Mike's brow furrowed. He shifted uncomfortably in his chair. This wasn't the first time she'd mentioned feeling unlucky or cursed, but the way she was speaking now, it was as if she truly believed it.

"Minow," he said gently, "that was a long time ago. You're not cursed. You're here now, with me and Itsada."

She barely seemed to hear him, her gaze fixed somewhere beyond him, her expression forlorn. "There were times I thought… maybe if I disappeared, everything would get better. Like when I jumped in the river as a little girl. I thought if I just… drifted away, no one would miss me."

Mike stiffened. "What do you mean, you jumped in a river?"

She nodded absently, a strange smile on her lips. "I must have been about eight or nine. It was the rainy season, and the river was swollen. I slipped in and let the current take me. I thought, 'This is it. This is how I disappear.' But the water spat me out, just like it did here, in England. It wouldn't let me go. Even the river didn't want me, Mike."

He felt a chill run down his spine. This was different from her usual rants about the "Thai Ninjas" or the supposed assassination attempts. This felt… darker, more personal.

He tried to steer the conversation back to safer ground.

"You know, painting might help you, Minow," he suggested, trying to sound casual. "Why don't you give it another go?"

For a while, it seemed like she might. She set up a small station in the dining room, brushes and paints scattered across the table. She'd sit there for hours, hunched over a canvas, her hand moving slowly, almost tentatively, as if she were trying to draw something buried deep within her memory.

But the results were always the same— simple, childlike shapes and colours. Houses with crooked roofs, stick figures with smiling faces, flowers that looked more like splatters of paint. Mike didn't have the heart to criticize her, but she could see the pity in his eyes.

"I'm no good at this, am I?" she murmured one day, staring at a painting of what seemed to be a sun and a house. "I paint like a little girl."

"It's fine, Minow. It's just for fun," Mike replied, forcing a smile. "It doesn't have to be perfect."

But she shook her head, frustration clouding her face. "No, it's not fine. I'm regressing, Mike. I'm… I'm going backwards. I feel like… I'm becoming a child again. What's happening to me?"

He didn't know what to say. Regression—was that what this was? He'd heard the term before, something to do with trauma or deep psychological issues, but he never imagined it would happen to Minow. Was this the next phase of her madness? He hadn't even considered that she might spiral into something different, something worse.

Days bled into weeks, and her stories became more erratic, more disjointed. One moment, she'd be recounting an incident at school where a teacher had scolded her in front of the class; the next, she'd be talking about how she'd convinced herself she was a bird and tried to fly off the roof of her house.

"Did you know I broke my arm once, jumping off the roof?" she asked out of the blue one afternoon.

Mike glanced up from his newspaper. "No, you never told me that."

"Mm-hmm," she nodded vigorously, almost childishly. "I thought if I flapped my arms hard enough, I'd fly. But I just fell… straight down. Splat!" She slapped her hand on the table, laughing lightly. But the laughter didn't reach her eyes.

"You're not a child, Minow," he said softly. "You're a grown woman. You have a son. You have me."

She looked at him then, her expression puzzled, as if she couldn't quite grasp what he was saying. "But I don't feel like a grown woman, Mike. I feel… small. Like I'm shrinking."

The helplessness in her voice made something inside him twist painfully. He reached out, covering her hand with his,

squeezing gently. "You're not shrinking.
You're still here. We'll get through this."

But even as he said the words, he knew they
were empty. He had no idea how to pull her
out of whatever dark place she'd fallen into.
He could only sit there, listening to her
endless stream of memories, watching her
grow more and more disconnected from
reality.

Minow stopped painting soon after that. The
canvases piled up in the corner of the room,
gathering dust. She stopped going outside,
stopped cooking, stopped everything that
hinted at normalcy. Instead, she'd sit on the
living room floor, her legs crossed, rocking
back and forth, her eyes vacant as she
murmured to herself about the bakery, the
river, the birds that never flew.

Mike stood in the doorway one evening,
watching her. He didn't know what to do,
how to help her. He felt useless, a spectator
to his wife's unravelling. He'd thought that
getting rid of her paranoia, her obsession
with the supposed assassins, would make

things better. But this… this was worse, somehow. It was like she was disappearing in front of him, slipping back into some shadowy corner of her mind that he couldn't reach.

"Minow, can you hear me?" he asked quietly.

She didn't respond, just kept murmuring, rocking back and forth like a child.

"Minow!" he tried again, louder this time.

Her head jerked up, her eyes wide and startled. For a moment, it looked like she didn't recognize him. But then she blinked, and a flicker of awareness returned.

"Mike?" she whispered, her voice small and scared. "What's happening to me?"

"I don't know," he admitted, his voice breaking. "But we'll figure it out. I promise."

But even as he made that promise, he felt a chill of doubt creep down his spine. Because deep down, he knew this was something far beyond his ability to fix.

Chapter Fifteen: The Start

It started on a night like any other.

The house was quiet, the oppressive stillness broken only by the ticking of the old grandfather clock downstairs. Mike shuffled through the dimly lit hallway, heading towards the kitchen for a glass of water. It was late—well past midnight—and the rest of the house was dark. As he walked past the bathroom, something caught his eye: the door was slightly ajar.

At first, he thought nothing of it. Minow was often careless, leaving things half-done, her mind too preoccupied to close a door or turn off a light. He moved to shut it, but just as his fingers touched the handle, he paused.

There was no light on inside, but the faint glow of the streetlamp outside seeped through the frosted window, casting a soft shadow on the tiled floor. Through the small opening, he could see the silhouette of Minow—sitting quietly on the toilet, her knees drawn up, her hair cascading over her shoulders in dark, tangled waves. It covered her bare breasts, giving her an almost ethereal, haunting look.

She was naked, her figure illuminated only by the faintest of outlines, every curve and contour visible in the half-light. Mike felt his breath catch in his throat. He hadn't seen her like this in years, hadn't felt this strange stirring of excitement and curiosity for... well, he couldn't remember how long. There was something about the vulnerability of the moment, the unintentional intimacy of it, that made him stop in his tracks.

He took a step back, retreating into the shadows of his own room across the narrow corridor. From there, he could still see her, the angle perfect enough to catch glimpses of her movements. She was completely unaware of his presence—lost in her own thoughts, her gaze distant as she sat there.

A pulse of something dark and thrilling rushed through him. It was as if he were watching a stranger, not the woman he'd been married to for nearly two decades. This version of Minow was raw, unfiltered, and somehow, it made her more beautiful than he'd ever remembered.

She shifted slightly, the movement causing her hair to part just enough for him to catch sight of the pale skin of her chest, the gentle rise and fall of her breathing. He felt his pulse quicken, a hot flush spreading across his face.

This was wrong—he knew it. He shouldn't be standing here, shouldn't be watching her like some perverted voyeur. But he couldn't tear himself away. He was mesmerized, his eyes glued to her like he was seeing her for the first time. He stepped back even further into his room, his heart pounding.

And then, the thought came to him: What if I filmed her?

It was like a whisper in the back of his mind, seductive and insistent. He shook his head, trying to dispel it, but the idea clung to him, growing stronger with every second he watched her. He knew the thought was twisted, knew it was a step beyond the boundaries of decency and respect. But in that moment, it didn't matter.

What was left to respect, anyway? Their marriage was a shell of what it once was— no love, no passion, just a hollow routine that they both went through out of some twisted sense of duty. He felt more like a caretaker than a husband, and she, a patient rather than a partner.

Slowly, almost as if in a trance, he pulled his phone out of his pocket. His hands shook slightly as he unlocked it, the soft glow of the screen casting a faint light in the darkened room. He hesitated, the rational part of his mind screaming at him to stop, to put the phone away, to go back to bed.

But he didn't. Instead, he swiped to the camera app, his thumb hovering over the record button. He glanced up one more time, checking to make sure she hadn't noticed him. Minow still sat there, her head bowed, the dark curtain of her hair hiding her face.

With a deep breath, he angled the phone towards the small opening of the bathroom door. His thumb pressed down, and the screen blinked red, the tiny numbers in the corner beginning to count up.

He filmed her for only a few seconds— thirty, maybe forty at most. The image on the screen was grainy, the lighting poor, but he could see her clearly enough. The delicate curve of her neck, the slender line of her back as she leaned forward slightly, the way her shoulders twitched as if shivering.

It was intoxicating, the thrill of doing something forbidden, the rush of adrenaline that coursed through him. When he finally stopped the recording, his hands were slick with sweat, his heart pounding so loudly he was sure she'd be able to hear it from across the hall.

He tucked the phone away, taking a step back into the shadows of his room. His chest heaved as he tried to calm himself, the reality of what he'd just done crashing down on him like a cold wave. He felt a twisted sense of satisfaction mixed with shame, the conflicting emotions warring inside him.

He sat down on the edge of his bed, staring blankly at the wall. What was he becoming? This wasn't him—he wasn't this kind of man. He'd always prided himself on being decent, respectful, but lately... lately, everything felt so blurred, so skewed.

Minow's illness had taken so much from him, from them. He'd lost the woman he'd once known, the vibrant, lively girl who'd captured his heart in the chaos of Bangkok's nightlife. Now, all that was left was this broken version of her, this sad, fragile creature who drifted through their house like a ghost. He'd been patient, tried to be understanding, but her madness, her obsession with the past—it had taken its toll on him.

He thought of the video stored on his phone, the brief clip of her sitting there, exposed and unaware. The image was burned into his mind, replaying over and over. He knew he shouldn't watch it again, but even as he thought that, he felt his hand drifting back towards his pocket, the urge to see her like that one more time nearly overwhelming.

What was he doing? What was he planning?

He took a deep breath, forcing himself to stand up, to move away from the phone. He wouldn't watch it tonight. He needed time to think, to understand what this strange compulsion was. He needed to clear his head, to get some perspective.

But even as he tried to rationalize, tried to convince himself that he'd just made a mistake, he couldn't shake the excitement that still buzzed under his skin. He couldn't deny the thrill he'd felt, the strange sense of power it had given him.

As he lay back down in bed, staring up at the ceiling, he made a decision. This would be the only time. He'd delete the video in the morning, pretend it had never happened.

He'd forget about this dark impulse and go back to being the man he used to be.

But deep down, he knew it wouldn't be that simple. Something had shifted between them tonight. A door had been opened that couldn't be easily closed. And as he closed his eyes, the faint outline of Minow's naked form still lingering behind his eyelids, he couldn't help but wonder what he would do if the opportunity presented itself again.

The plan was already forming in the back of his mind, a shadowy idea that both thrilled and repelled him in equal measure.

Because he knew, without a doubt, that there would be a next time.

Chapter Sixteen: Movie

The idea simmered in Mike's mind for days, refusing to leave him alone. It occupied his thoughts when he was at work, seeped into his dreams at night, and lingered like a tantalizing whisper in the back of his head. He found himself glancing at Minow more often watching her with a different kind of intensity, searching for the perfect moment to capture her on camera again. He wasn't sure when the plan had become so detailed in his mind, but now that it had taken root, it felt inevitable.

The original thought—telling her he wanted to make a film—faded quickly. There was no way she'd agree. She'd probably scoff, roll her eyes, maybe even get angry, thinking it was another one of his attempts to control or manipulate her. No, that approach would never work.

It wasn't just about seeing her on camera. It was about the thrill of watching her unknowingly, the forbidden nature of the act. He wanted to capture her as she was— unguarded, unaware, vulnerable. The kind of raw beauty and authenticity that no staged performance could ever replicate.

He imagined how he'd do it: filming her through the crack of a door as she wandered around the house in one of her loose-fitting T-shirts, the hem swaying around her thighs, teasing him with fleeting glimpses of skin. He thought about those worn, little black shorts she liked to wear—how they clung to her hips and rode up with every step. He envisioned her scrubbing the floor, cooking in the kitchen, or even just sitting on the couch staring blankly at the TV. The mundane, everyday moments were what excited him most. It was his own private film, a voyeuristic project that existed solely for his pleasure.

But the idea didn't stop there.

He also wanted to capture himself—his reactions, his face as he peeked around corners or watched her through a slightly open window. He wanted to document the thrill, the excitement, and the way his pulse raced with each stolen glance. The film wasn't just about her; it was about them. His gaze would become another character in the story—something omnipresent, always watching, always waiting.

Mike knew he had to be careful, though. If she caught him… No, he couldn't let himself think like that. He wouldn't get caught. He'd been careful the first time, hadn't he? He'd made sure she hadn't noticed. And he'd be even more cautious from now on.

He spent the next few days meticulously planning. First, he positioned small cameras around the house, hidden discreetly behind objects that wouldn't draw attention. He bought a few online, nothing too fancy—just enough to get clear footage. One was placed behind the stack of books on the living room shelf, its lens peeking out between the spines. Another was perched on top of the kitchen cabinet, angled downwards to capture a wide shot of the room.

His favourite setup, though, was in their bedroom. He'd installed a tiny camera inside a decorative vase that sat on top of her dresser, the lens pointed directly at the bed. He tested it multiple times, ensuring it would pick up every subtle movement, every shift of her body as she lay down or changed clothes.

But that was just one part of the plan. The second phase was more delicate.

He needed to film himself, too—show the contrast between his own anticipation and her unawareness. So, he set up a camera in his own room, aimed at the door leading out into the hall. He'd record himself sitting on the bed, watching through a crack in the door as she moved about. It felt perverse, even to him, but he couldn't deny the surge of excitement that came with it.

Then he waited.

Days passed without incident. Minow moved about the house in her usual routine, rarely straying from her designated safe spaces: the kitchen, the bedroom, the living room. Most of the time, she stayed in bed, her movements slow and lethargic. She'd spend hours staring at the ceiling, lost in her own thoughts. Even the usual moments he looked forward to—seeing her in those shorts, her hair loose around her shoulders— were rare now. She mostly wore sweatpants and oversized sweaters, hiding her body as if ashamed of it.

But he was patient. He knew she'd break the monotony eventually. And then, he'd be ready.

One evening, the opportunity finally presented itself. Mike was in the living room, pretending to watch TV, when he heard the soft creak of the bedroom door opening. He looked up, holding his breath. Minow stepped out hesitantly, dressed in one of his old white T-shirts. It hung loosely on her small frame, the fabric so worn and thin that he could see the outline of her body through it. The hem barely brushed the tops of her thighs.

He watched, heart hammering in his chest, as she moved silently down the hallway and into the kitchen. His eyes followed her every step, noting how her bare feet seemed to barely make a sound on the wooden floorboards.

This was it.

Mike slipped his phone out of his pocket, activating the camera feed from the hidden cameras. The kitchen view flickered to life on his screen, showing her standing by the counter, her back to him. She reached up to grab something from a cupboard, the motion causing the T-shirt to rise just enough to expose the lower curve of her backside. He swallowed hard, his fingers tightening around the phone.

He needed to film himself watching her, to complete the scene. Moving quickly and quietly, he crept back to his room, positioning himself so that he could see her through the slightly open door. He hit record on the camera set up in his room, making sure it was angled perfectly to catch his expression.

There she was, still in the kitchen, oblivious to his gaze. He stared at her, a mix of guilt and desire churning in his stomach. The footage on his phone showed her reaching for a glass, her movements slow and deliberate. Then, suddenly, she stopped.

For a moment, he thought she'd sensed him—his breath hitched, and he nearly dropped the phone. But she only turned slightly, glancing at something on the counter before continuing her task. He exhaled softly, relief flooding through him.

This was it—the beginning of his project. He'd wait for more moments like this, piecing together the footage bit by bit until he had his film. He didn't know what it would become, or even why he was doing it. He just knew he had to. It was a compulsion now, an obsession that he couldn't shake.

As he sat there, the camera capturing his wide-eyed stare, a thought crossed his mind: Was this the way he'd reconnect with her? Was this what their marriage had been reduced to—a twisted game of cat and mouse, with him as the hunter and her the unknowing prey?

He didn't know. He didn't care.

Because as long as he had that screen between them—those cameras separating his voyeuristic pleasure from the reality of what he was doing—he could pretend this wasn't a violation. He could convince himself that this was just another form of intimacy, a way to feel closer to the woman he'd once loved.

The thrill of it was undeniable. And the thrill, he realized, was all he had left.

Chapter Seventeen: Screenplay

The more Mike filmed, the more the obsession grew. It started subtly small, careful captures here and there. A slight creak in the bathroom door and he'd be at the ready, his GoPro in hand, recording Minow as she moved around, oblivious to his gaze. He recorded her stepping into the shower, her hands moving through her hair, the water cascading down her bare back. He filmed her undressing in front of the mirror, catching the momentary glimpse of her skin before she slipped into a loose-fitting T-shirt and old shorts.

There was no screenplay, no outline or plot to follow. Just random shots pieced together by his desire, each one fuelled by the thrill of her unawareness. His "film" wasn't really a film at all—just a series of voyeuristic clips, each more intimate than the last.

Mike found himself watching her like a predator stalking prey, biding his time, waiting for the right moments to pounce. When she left the bedroom door open a crack, he'd linger just outside, camera in hand, capturing her lying on the bed or folding clothes in her usual sluggish way. Whenever she went into the bathroom to change or wash up, he'd stand outside the door, holding the camera at just the right angle to catch glimpses of her body. There were times when she'd move too quickly, when the footage came out blurry or unfocused, but Mike didn't care. He could always get another shot.

It wasn't like there was any shortage of opportunities. Minow seemed to live in her own little world, disconnected from reality. She'd wander aimlessly around the house, muttering under her breath or occasionally breaking into laughter. Those were the moments that disturbed Mike the most—not the laughter itself, but the fact that nothing seemed to trigger it. It was like she was reacting to something only she could see, something that existed solely in her mind.

He'd captured a few of those unsettling moments, too. In one clip, she stood in the kitchen, giggling softly as she stared out the window. There was nothing outside—no bird or squirrel or person to make her laugh. But she smiled like she'd just heard the funniest joke, her shoulders shaking with silent laughter. Mike had zoomed in on her face, hoping to catch a glimpse of what was going on behind those dark eyes.

There was nothing. Just that vacant, faraway look.

Other times, she'd whisper to herself—fragments of conversations that made no sense. "It's not right… They know… Don't tell him… Cursed, all cursed…" Mike recorded it all, fascinated and repelled at the same time. It felt like he was documenting her descent into madness, each frame a step further away from the woman she used to be.

He even started naming the clips in his private collection. "Shower Scene 1," "Bedroom – Undressing," "Laughing in Kitchen." Each one labelled and dated, a record of his twisted documentary.

One morning, he caught her standing in front of the bathroom mirror, wearing nothing but a towel wrapped around her waist. The GoPro was set up on the countertop, hidden behind a pile of magazines. She was brushing her hair, staring at her reflection with that same blank expression. He watched through the tiny screen of his phone, the camera feed flickering as she moved.

Then, out of nowhere, she dropped the brush and leaned in closer to the mirror, pressing her forehead against the glass. Mike's heart skipped a beat. He zoomed in, holding his breath as she whispered something he couldn't quite make out.

"Stop looking," she murmured, her voice low and tremulous.

Mike froze, his finger hovering over the record button. Had she seen him? Had she realized what he was doing? For a moment, panic surged through him. He imagined her turning, her eyes locking onto the camera, catching him in the act.

But she didn't. She just stayed there, staring at her own reflection, her lips moving silently. He leaned forward, trying to catch the next words, but they were too quiet. Her hand came up, pressing against the mirror like she was reaching for someone on the other side.

"Please… make them stop."

The hairs on the back of Mike's neck stood on end. Who was she talking to? Did she think someone was watching her from the mirror? Was this another manifestation of her paranoia? He kept recording, mesmerized by the scene unfolding before him.

Then, as quickly as it had started, it was over. Minow straightened up, blinking as if she'd just woken from a dream. She glanced around the bathroom, and for one horrifying second, Mike thought her gaze would land on the GoPro.

But she turned away, dropping the towel to the floor and stepping into the shower. The sound of water hitting tile filled the room, and Mike exhaled softly, his heart pounding.

He reviewed the footage later that night, replaying it over and over again. Something about the way she'd looked at herself in the mirror unnerved him. It was like she'd seen something in her own reflection that scared her. He tried to dismiss it, telling himself it was just another one of her episodes, but the image stayed with him long after he'd shut off the camera.

The next few days were more of the same. He continued filming whenever the opportunity arose, capturing her as she moved through the house, oblivious to his presence. The thrill was still there, but it was starting to feel… different. The more footage he collected, the more detached he felt. He was no longer just an observer; he was a participant in her unravelling, documenting her every breakdown, every moment of despair.

One evening, while reviewing a recent clip of her sitting on the bed, rocking back and forth, he caught sight of his own reflection in the screen. He didn't recognize the man staring back at him—eyes wide, mouth slightly open, a look of rapt fascination on his face. He looked like a stranger.

"What the hell am I doing?" he muttered, his voice sounding hollow in the empty room.

But he didn't stop. He couldn't. He told himself he was just keeping an eye on her, making sure she didn't hurt herself again. That's all it was. A way to keep her safe. He wasn't doing anything wrong. He wasn't exploiting her. This was for her own good.

Yet, deep down, he knew that was a lie. He wasn't filming to protect her. He was filming because he wanted to, because the sight of her like this—the raw, unfiltered reality of her—had become his new addiction.

And like all addictions, it was getting harder to control. Harder to stop.

Chapter 15: The Screenplay

The days blurred together, one indistinguishable from the next, as Mike meticulously edited his film. He spent countless hours alone in the spare room, hunched over his desk, the soft glow of the monitor casting a sickly light across his weary face. Each clip, each scene, was cut and spliced with a care that bordered on obsession. The footage had become more than just a collection of stolen moments—it was his escape, his twisted form of control over a world spiralling out of reach.

He titled it *Forbidden Fruit*, a name that encapsulated both the allure and the taboo nature of his hidden project. The entire film was constructed from the shadows, pieced together with shaky footage of Minow's unguarded, vulnerable moments. A voyeuristic compilation of her bare existence: from the mundane routines of scrubbing floors and washing dishes to more intimate, unsettling sequences where she wandered half-dressed, lost in her own thoughts, seemingly unaware of his gaze lingering on her.

And then, there was the ending—the scene that had haunted Mike ever since he'd captured it. The final shot of Minow's lifeless body in the bathtub, the water stained red, the silence suffocating. It was a moment that seared itself into his mind, and yet, he couldn't bring himself to delete it. The image was burned into his psyche, a reminder of how far things had gone, how far he had let them go.

This wasn't just a film anymore. It was a window into the decay of their marriage, a portrayal of how Minow's sanity had slipped through her fingers as easily as she had slipped through his.

Mike stared at the final cut of the film, his finger hovering over the play button. Showing the world this project was out of the question—it was his secret, his forbidden fruit. But maybe, just maybe, he could share it with her.

He wondered how she would react, whether seeing herself through his lens would evoke any emotion at all. Would she scream? Would she cry? Or worse… would she just stare blankly at the screen, uncomprehending, like she often did now?

It was a risk, but it didn't matter. He had to show her. He needed her to see.

Taking a deep breath, Mike saved the file, labelling it as "*Forbidden Fruit: The Unseen Minow*". Then, he placed the edited version onto a USB drive. He glanced at the clock—it was nearing midnight, and the house was silent except for the faint hum of the refrigerator down the hall.

He knew she'd be awake. She rarely slept anymore, lost as she was in a haze of her past, mumbling to herself about things that no longer existed. Perhaps this would bring her back, he thought. Perhaps seeing herself, seeing the pain and madness captured so plainly, would shock her into recognizing what she had become.

With a final glance at the screen, he pocketed the USB and headed towards Minow's bedroom, where the thin sliver of light underneath the door signalled her insomnia.

Tonight, he would show her the truth—the truth of what she was to him now. A subject. An object. His muse, broken and beautiful.

Mike took a deep breath and knocked gently on the door, holding the written 'screenplay' ready to show his work.

Screenplay: *Forbidden Fruit*

Genre: Psychological Drama
Duration: ~12 minutes

Setting: Mike's Home, Various Rooms
Characters:

1. **Mike** (late 50s, British, greying hair, unkempt, looks tense and detached)

2. **Minow** (early 40s, Thai, fragile, lost in her own thoughts, movements languid and absent)

FADE IN:

INT. BATHROOM - NIGHT

Soft, ambient music hums in the background. The camera is positioned behind the door, slightly ajar. The angle is low, framing the doorway in a voyeuristic manner. A subtle beam of light from a streetlamp outside falls into the room, casting a dim glow.

Mike's silhouette is visible in the foreground. He leans closer, peeking through the narrow crack of the door.

CUT TO:

Minow sits on the edge of the bathtub, her hair covering her face, falling over her bare shoulders. She wears nothing but a loose, white T-shirt, wet and clinging to her skin, revealing more than concealing. Her fingers trail absently in the water.

Mike's POV shifts slightly as he adjusts his view. His breathing is audible, controlled but shallow.

Minow stands up, her movements slow, almost trance-like. The camera stays with Mike's gaze, focusing on her figure as she bends down, the hem of the shirt riding up her thighs.

CUT TO:

INT. BATHROOM - DAY (FLASHBACK)

Minow is on her hands and knees, scrubbing the tiled floor. She wears the same loose T-shirt and small black shorts. A large puddle of water reflects the afternoon sunlight. As she leans forward, a side view reveals a hint of her breast through the loose neckline.

The camera captures her in close-up from above, emphasizing her vulnerable position. Her hands move mechanically, dipping the rag in the water and wringing it out. A faint smile plays on her lips, though her eyes are vacant.

Mike's shadow appears on the wall as he steps closer, filming with his GoPro.

CUT TO:

INT. BEDROOM - DAY

Minow stands by the window, staring outside at nothing in particular. She is in a short, floral-patterned dress. A breeze from the open window causes the fabric to ripple against her legs. She sighs deeply.

Mike's hand appears, sliding the camera lens through the barely open door. He zooms in, capturing the way her dress clings to her body.

SFX: The faint clicks of the camera focusing.

Minow shifts, turning her head slightly, as if sensing something. The camera pulls back quickly, the image blurs, and the frame cuts to black.

CUT TO:

INT. KITCHEN - EARLY EVENING

Minow hums softly, chopping vegetables. Her hair is tied up in a loose bun, strands falling messily around her face. She wears a simple tank top and pyjama shorts.

Mike's POV is from outside the kitchen door. He films her from a distance. The focus shifts from her bare shoulder to the knife in her hand.

The blade glints under the kitchen light as she slices through a carrot. Her hands move slowly, deliberately. The humming stops abruptly.

She pauses, staring down at the knife, then glances sideways toward the door. Mike's camera pulls back slightly, adjusting to capture her reaction.

CUT TO:

INT. LIVING ROOM - LATE NIGHT

Minow lies on the couch, curled up in a foetal position, staring at a blank TV screen. She's wearing an oversized sweater and nothing else. Her bare legs are visible, knees pulled up to her chest.

Mike films her from across the room, the camera hidden behind a shelf of books. He zooms in on her face. Her lips move silently, mouthing something incoherent.

The camera pans down slowly, capturing the way her fingers dig into the fabric of the couch, gripping it tightly.

SFX: A soft whimper escapes her.

CUT TO:

INT. BATHROOM - NIGHT (FINAL SCENE)

The room is dimly lit, a single flickering candle casting dancing shadows on the walls.

Minow lies in the bathtub, completely still. The camera pans slowly up her body, starting from her feet submerged in the water, moving up her legs, then her torso. The water is murky, tinted red.

Mike's hand shakes slightly as he holds the camera, the frame trembling. He steps closer.

Minow's left arm dangles over the edge of the tub. A razor blade lies on the floor beneath her hand, a crimson stain trailing from her wrist to the water.

The camera zooms in on her face. Her eyes are closed, lips slightly parted as if she's sleeping. Her hair fans out, floating around her like a dark halo.

SFX: Mike's breath catches in his throat. He steps back, the camera dipping downward as he struggles to steady himself.

CUT TO:

The shot changes abruptly, showing Mike's reflection in the bathroom mirror, his face pale and expressionless. He holds the camera to his chest, staring at the scene before him.

For a long moment, there is only silence. Then, he turns off the camera, and the screen goes black.

FADE OUT.

END CREDITS:

Soft music plays as the credits roll. The title "Forbidden Fruit" appears in elegant, serif letters, dissolving slowly into the dark screen.

Chapter 16: The Call

The bathroom was a blur of stark white tiles splattered with red. Mike stood over Minow's body, the small bathroom suddenly feeling cavernous and empty. The GoPro, hastily pushed into his back pocket, dug into his hip, but he barely noticed the discomfort. His mind was a static hum, every coherent thought drowned out by the image of

Minow's pale, lifeless form slumped in his arms.

He cradled her limp body, her dark hair slick and heavy against his chest, strands sticking to his shirt, wet and tangled. The water that had sloshed over the edge of the tub pooled at his feet, mingling with the deep crimson of her blood. For a moment, he felt paralyzed—unable to move, unable to comprehend what to do next.

"Minow," he whispered, his voice breaking. He shook her gently, as if she could be roused from this state by the sound of her name. But her eyes remained shut, the dark crescents of her lashes brushing her cheeks, eerily serene.

He looked down at the deep gashes on her wrists, the lines of severed skin so precise they almost seemed surgical. The blood no longer gushed but trickled, a slow, dark ooze. It smeared his hands, sticky and warm, and Mike felt a wave of nausea rise in his throat. He had filmed her in every vulnerable moment, but now, confronted with the reality of her frailty, he was lost.

The decision to call the police came not from rational thought but from instinct, his hand reaching for the phone in his pocket, slick with her blood. The buttons slipped under his fingers as he dialled 999, his heart pounding in his ears. Each ring felt like a lifetime.

"Emergency services. Which service do you require?"

"Ambulance… and the police," he stammered, his voice strained and hollow. "It's my wife… She—she's in the bath. She cut her wrists. There's—there's blood everywhere."

"Stay calm, sir. Is she breathing?"

Mike glanced down at Minow's face, so still, so peaceful. He couldn't see any rise and fall in her chest, no sign of life. Panic surged through him like an electric current.

"I—I don't know. I don't think so," he choked out.

"Help is on the way, sir. Stay on the line with me. Can you try checking for a pulse?"

A pulse. The simplest thing, and yet his hands trembled as he shifted Minow's weight, one hand fumbling to press against the delicate skin of her neck. There was no steady beat, no reassuring thrum of life beneath his fingertips. Just silence.

"There's nothing," he whispered.

"Okay, sir. Keep her head elevated and stay with her until the paramedics arrive. They'll be there soon."

The call ended, and Mike let the phone drop to the floor with a soft clatter. He stood there, holding Minow's cold body, the weight of her sagging against him. What should he do now? How could he possibly make this right?

Minutes passed, or maybe hours—time lost all meaning. The house was eerily silent, the only sound the faint dripping of water from Minow's arm as it dangled over the edge of the tub, fingers curled inward like she was reaching for something only she could see.

And then there was noise—footsteps, voices, the front door swinging open with a crash.

"Mr. Anders? Where are you?" a voice called out, echoing through the hallway.

"Here… in here!" Mike shouted back, his voice strained and hoarse.

The bathroom door was thrown wide open, and a team of paramedics flooded the small space. Mike stepped back, releasing his hold on Minow, and she slid back into the water with a sickening splash. He stumbled, almost falling as he was pushed aside.

He watched, numb and detached, as the paramedics moved with swift efficiency. Hands pressed against Minow's chest, tubes and wires materialized from nowhere, the soft hiss of oxygen mingling with the sterile scent of medical equipment.

A police officer stood beside Mike, a young woman with kind eyes and a firm grip on his arm.

"Mr. Anders, I'm Officer Lewis. You need to step outside, okay? Let the medics do their work."

Mike nodded, though he barely registered her words. He let himself be guided out of the bathroom, his eyes fixed on the chaotic scene of flashing lights and urgent voices. The world seemed to tilt, everything slipping out of focus. The officer sat him down on the edge of his bed, and he could hear her speaking, but the words were distant, muffled.

"…tell me what happened, Mr. Anders."

"I… I found her like that," he murmured, his gaze drifting to the blood smeared on his hands. "She was just… there. I didn't know what to do."

He looked up, meeting the officer's gaze for the first time. Her expression was sympathetic but guarded, a look he'd seen countless times in his career. The look of someone trying to balance empathy with suspicion.

"Did she say anything to you, before it happened? Anything at all?"

Mike blinked slowly, trying to piece together the fragmented memories of the past few days, but it was all a blur. The only thing that stood out was that last scene—Minow's lifeless body, just as he'd captured it on camera. He swallowed hard, the image burned into his mind.

"No... nothing," he finally whispered.

The officer nodded, making a few notes. "We're going to need to ask you some more questions, but for now, just take a moment to breathe. The paramedics will do everything they can."

Mike glanced back at the bathroom door, where they were still working on Minow, the air thick with urgency. He closed his eyes, willing himself to stay calm. But the truth was, he had no idea what to feel. Relief? Guilt? Fear?

All he knew was that he was standing on the precipice of something terrible, something he'd unwittingly set in motion. And there was no turning back now.

Chapter 17: Forbidden Fruit's Final Cut

The house was suffocatingly quiet. The kind of quiet that seemed to pulse against Mike's temples, reminding him with every beat that Minow was gone and the life they'd known together—chaotic, fractured, but shared—was over.

Mike sat alone in the dimly lit living room, a single glass of whiskey balanced on the armrest beside him. The flickering glow from the screen was the only light in the room, casting long shadows across the walls. He stared at the paused image, his finger hovering over the play button, hesitant.

"Forbidden Fruit."

That's what he'd called it. A title that held a grim irony, now more than ever. The footage had been pieced together meticulously, each shot a voyeuristic glimpse into their broken lives. It was raw, unfiltered, and disturbingly honest. But the final scene... the final scene was something else entirely.

Mike took a deep breath and hit play.

The film began as it always did—with the soft creak of the bathroom door, the shot framed through a sliver of the door's opening. Minow, in her loose T-shirt and tiny shorts, on her hands and knees mopping the water off the bathroom floor. Her hair cascaded down, hiding her face, but there was a grace in the way she moved, even in the most mundane of tasks. That was how the film unfolded—Minow unaware of his presence, captured in stolen moments: dressing, undressing, bathing, all the while shrouded in an unspoken sadness.

As the minutes ticked by, Mike found himself pulled into the story, the layers of their twisted relationship revealed in every frame. The critics had praised the film for its depth, its audacity. They called it a "haunting exploration of isolation and obsession." But Mike knew better. It was a confession—a document of his obsession, his desperation to hold onto something that had slipped through his fingers long ago.

The accolades had poured in: Best Screenplay at The Los Angeles Arthouse Film Critics Awards, a nod from the Venice International Short Film Festival, even a mention at Sundance. For a film with such unsettling content, it had resonated deeply with audiences and critics alike. They saw it as a bold artistic statement. He knew it for what it truly was— a voyeur's journal, thinly veiled as art.

The scene shifted, the camera now angled from behind the bathroom mirror, capturing Minow as she slipped out of her clothes and stepped into the tub. Steam rose around her, the water rippling softly as she submerged herself. Mike's hands tightened around the remote. He knew what was coming next.

In the original version, he had edited the footage to end just as Minow leaned back against the tub, her eyes closed, a soft smile playing on her lips. It was a poignant image, full of aching beauty and sorrow. But that wasn't the truth.

The truth was in the unedited version, the one no one had seen. The version he hadn't dared to submit to the festivals. Because in that version, the scene didn't end with Minow's smile.

The camera lingered as Minow's hand slipped under the water, a flash of metal glinting in the dim light. He'd never shown anyone that cut, where she slowly drew the blade across her wrist, crimson spiralling through the bathwater like ink spreading through milk. He'd never shared the footage of her going limp, the tub transforming into a macabre painting of life seeping away.

He took another sip of whiskey, the burn traveling down his throat, grounding him in the present. His finger hesitated over the mouse, the cursor hovering over the file labelled "Final Cut – Unreleased". A part of him itched to watch it again, to relive that moment in its entirety.

But he couldn't. Not even now.

The edited version had been enough for the critics. Enough to win him praise, acclaim, validation for the madness that had consumed him. They'd seen the art in his obsession, not the horror.

Yet something nagged at him, something hollow. He'd won awards, yes, but he couldn't help feeling like he was hiding the true climax of the story. The missing piece that held the raw, unvarnished truth.

He glanced at the stack of certificates on the table beside him. "Best Director," "Best Cinematography," "Audience Choice Award"—all hollow words, empty accolades. He had poured his soul into this film, bared the ugliest parts of himself, and still, it wasn't enough.

The critics had applauded the ambiguity of the ending, the restraint he'd shown in not exploiting Minow's final moments. But it wasn't restraint. It was cowardice.

What would they think if they saw the real ending? If they saw the full truth? He could almost hear the clamour, the outraged shock, the retraction of awards. Or maybe—just maybe—it would cement his legacy as a filmmaker willing to go where no one else dared.

The idea was intoxicating. He leaned forward, his hand hovering over the play button.

But then he heard her voice. Not in reality—no, she was long gone. But in his mind, Minow's laughter, the way she would giggle softly to herself, lost in her own world. He thought of that last night, the blood swirling through the water, her life slipping away while he'd stood there, helpless.

What good would showing that to the world do now? It wouldn't bring her back. It wouldn't make the silence in the house any less deafening.

He paused the film again, his gaze lingering on Minow's face frozen on the screen. The smile that never should have been the final image. Slowly, deliberately, he moved the cursor to the "Delete" option.

He hesitated, then clicked.

The screen went black.

The awards, the praise, the recognition—it all felt meaningless without her. In the end, he'd only been able to capture her essence on film, never in real life. The Minow on the screen was just a shadow of the woman she'd been.

Mike took one last look at the empty screen, then closed the laptop. He rose, his joints stiff, and wandered through the silent house, the echo of his footsteps a reminder of everything he'd lost.

Maybe it was time to let her go. Time to stop reliving those moments through the lens of a camera and face the reality he'd helped create.

But as he stood at the doorway of the empty bathroom, the lingering scent of blood and despair still haunting the air, he knew it wasn't that simple.

Some stories, once told, refused to let go.

Chapter 18: Return to Whoredom

The hum of the airplane engines droned on, lulling most of the passengers into a state of half-sleep. But not Mike. He sat rigidly in his seat, his gaze locked on the seatback in front of him, his thoughts miles away. In his lap, a small jar rested securely in his grip, nestled in a padded velvet pouch.

Minow's ashes.

After the funeral, the house had become unbearable. Each room echoed with her absence. He had moved through it like a ghost, opening cupboards and closets only to find her scent lingering faintly on old clothes and pillows. It was too much. Too empty.

So he'd made the decision—to take her back to where it had all started. To the chaotic streets of Bangkok, where he'd first seen her walk into that bar on Soi 11. Back to the place she'd always considered home, no matter how far she'd gone.

The flight attendant passed by, offering him a polite smile that he barely registered. He gave a slight nod in return and glanced down at the pouch. Next to it, on the empty seat, was his GoPro camera. The same one he'd used to film Forbidden Fruit. He reached out and ran a finger over the familiar contours of the device. It had been weeks since he'd last touched it. Weeks since he'd deleted the final cut of the film.

But then the ideas had started again whispering in the back of his mind. They always did. This time, though, it wasn't about Minow's brokenness. It was about closure. His closure.

A new short film. He didn't have a title yet, but he could already see the shots forming in his mind. The sprawling cityscape of Bangkok at night, neon lights casting a surreal glow. The crowded alleys of Patpong and the deserted backstreets of Soi 13, where he used to live. He would visit the old places, the memories embedded in every corner. The bar where they'd first met, the clubs where he'd spent nights lost in a haze of alcohol and lust. Each scene would be a chapter, a reflection of how everything had changed—and yet stayed the same.

And then there would be the final shot—him, standing at the Chao Phraya River, scattering her ashes into the murky water. A symbolic act of letting go. Of saying goodbye.

But that wasn't all. He had a darker idea lurking in the recesses of his mind. One he wasn't sure he'd actually follow through with, but it gnawed at him nonetheless. What if he retraced their steps—every place they'd been together—and filmed himself, not as a husband or lover, but as the voyeur? Watching her even now, from a distance, as if she were still there.

The screenplay he'd started writing detailed it all. The camera would follow a lone figure—him—wandering through the city, juxtaposed against footage of Minow, taken from the original film. Past and present colliding. Reality and memory blurring.

But was he ready to do that? To turn Minow's death into yet another artistic project?

He shook his head slightly, trying to dislodge the thoughts. It didn't matter right now. What mattered was getting her home.

"Sir, would you like anything to drink?" The flight attendant's voice cut through his reverie. Mike looked up, blinking as if waking from a dream.

"Whiskey. Neat," he replied, his voice rough. As she nodded and moved on, he glanced out the window at the vast expanse of sky, the sun dipping low on the horizon. They were getting close.

He closed his eyes and let himself drift, memories of Bangkok flooding back unbidden. The oppressive heat of the city at midday. The cacophony of street vendors and the ever-present hum of traffic. The smell of fried food, exhaust fumes, and jasmine.

He remembered how Minow's face would light up when they walked through the night markets, her fingers trailing over the colourful fabrics and trinkets. How she'd negotiate with the vendors, her voice rising in mock outrage before both parties burst into laughter. He remembered her sitting beside him on the rooftop bars, looking out over the skyline, a content smile on her face—back when she was happy, before everything had unravelled.

"Your drink, sir."

Mike opened his eyes and took the glass, nodding his thanks. He downed it in one go, the alcohol burning a path down his throat. It didn't help.

He looked back at the GoPro. Was it sick that he was even considering filming this trip? Maybe. Probably. But this was who he was now. The grieving husband. The failed protector. The man who turned his own tragedies into art.

Slowly, he unscrewed the cap of the jar, peering inside. The ashes were fine and pale, almost like powder. How could everything that had been Minow—her laughter, her anger, her sadness—be reduced to this? Just a handful of dust.

"I'm taking you home, Minow," he whispered. "One last time."

He'd visit the old places; pay homage to the memories they'd made. Maybe he'd even see some of the old faces—if they were still around. Mama San, the DJ she used to hang out with, the girls who'd laughed and flirted with him back in the day. Would they even remember him? Would they care?

The plane started its descent, and Mike tightened his grip on the jar. His heart thudded with a strange mix of anticipation and dread. He was going back to where it had all started, but he wasn't the same man anymore. And Minow… she wasn't the same either.

He leaned back and closed his eyes, imagining the opening shot of his new film. The camera panning over the skyline of Bangkok, the city lights flickering like a heartbeat. Then a cut to him, standing alone in the midst of it all, holding the jar. A man haunted by the past, trying to find closure in a place that had never offered anything but emptiness and deceit.

Maybe it was madness. Maybe it was art.

Or maybe it was just his way of saying goodbye.

As the wheels touched down on the tarmac, Mike took a deep breath. He was ready to begin filming again. But this time, he wasn't making a film about Minow's pain.

He was making a film about his own.

Chapter 19: Unscripted Nights

The sultry air of Bangkok enveloped Mike as he stepped out of the taxi on Sukhumvit Road. The chaotic energy of the city surged around him, a familiar mix of honking cars, buzzing tuk-tuks, and the chattering of vendors lining the sidewalk. He adjusted the strap of his backpack, feeling the weight of his concealed GoPro inside. The equipment was small, but it felt heavy against his chest—a constant reminder of his purpose.

He had spent the afternoon with Minow's family, handing over the jar of ashes, exchanging words he barely understood. Their faces were a blend of sorrow and acceptance. He had expected more—anger, accusations, something that would absolve him of the guilt gnawing at his insides. But they had been kind, too kind, offering him a seat at their table and a meal. It was suffocating. The familiar smell of Thai spices and incense brought back too many memories of a life he'd tried to forget.

Afterward, he had escaped to the streets. Now he found himself alone, wandering the city he once ruled like a king. He took a deep breath, his eyes scanning the skyline lit with neon signs. Everything felt different, yet the same. The Pickled Liver, the bar where he and Minow had celebrated the most significant—and disastrous—moments of their life, was gone. In its place, a soulless 7-Eleven stared back at him, its bright fluorescent lights casting an eerie glow on the street.

"Guess you can't go home again, huh?" he muttered to himself, shaking his head.

He made his way down Soi 11, where memories of drunken nights and laughter seemed to cling to the very bricks of the buildings. But they were just memories now. The girly bar where he'd first met Minow was shuttered and dark, a "For Sale" sign plastered on its dusty windows. Frustration simmered in his chest. The city had moved on without him, erasing the markers of his past.

He turned back onto the main road, weaving through the throng of tourists and locals. His feet carried him towards Soi 4, Nana Plaza—Bangkok's notorious adult playground. If there was any place where he could find a trace of his old life, it would be here. The neon lights flickered overhead, illuminating the narrow alley crammed with bars, street food vendors, and half-dressed women leaning against doorways, their voices mixing in a chorus of invitations.

The familiar thumping bass of pop music greeted him as he stepped inside the Plaza. He slipped the GoPro out of his backpack, concealing it inside his shirt. His pulse quickened as he switched it on, a soft buzz confirming it was recording. He didn't have a script, didn't know what he was looking for. But that was the thrill of it, wasn't it? The unpredictability.

He made his way through the maze of bars, his eyes scanning the faces of the girls lounging on stools and dancing on platforms. He doubted he'd recognize anyone after all these years, but he looked anyway. The girls all seemed younger now, dressed in tighter, more revealing outfits than he remembered. Each one flashed him a practiced smile, eyes sizing him up as they calculated his worth.

Mike stopped at a bar on the corner, ordering a Singha beer. He took a sip, savouring the bitter taste as he watched the scene unfold around him. Just like old times, he thought. Except there was no Minow to take home at the end of the night. No drunken laughter or whispered promises. Just him, alone.

"Tao rai?" he asked, testing his rusty Thai on a girl who had sidled up to him. She was stunning—dark hair framing a delicate face, her eyes sharp and calculating.

"Three thousand for short time," she replied, her accent smooth and practiced. "But you look like you want something… different."

Mike's pulse jumped. Did he look that desperate? That out of place? He shrugged it off, forcing a smile. "What's your name?"

"Cherry," she said, leaning closer. "I'm a model." She smiled, revealing perfect white teeth. There was something about her—her face, her poise—that reminded him of the girls who used to frequent the clubs with their HiSo patrons. She didn't belong here, in this seedy bar. And that's what drew him in.

"Let's get out of here," he said, sliding a few crisp bills into her hand. It was more than she'd asked for, but he didn't care.

Cherry's eyes widened slightly, but she quickly masked her surprise, slipping the money into her bra. "Okay, mister. Your hotel or mine?"

"Mine."

They left the bar and wove through the crowd, her arm linked through his. He felt the familiar rush of adrenaline, his mind already racing through potential shots for his new film. Cherry was perfect—poised and elegant, yet clearly out of place in this world. He could work with that. As they walked, he kept the GoPro running, capturing the way the neon lights reflected off her skin, the nervous glance she cast over her shoulder.

They reached his hotel, a modest place off Sukhumvit, far removed from the luxury suites he used to rent. He unlocked the door, holding it open as Cherry stepped inside, her heels clicking softly on the tiled floor. She glanced around, her gaze lingering on the bed, the small table cluttered with empty bottles, and then back to him.

"You want drink first?" she asked, already reaching for the minibar.

"No." His voice was low, almost a growl. "Just… relax."

She raised an eyebrow but complied, slipping off her shoes and sinking onto the bed. Mike moved quickly, positioning the GoPro on the dresser where it had a clear view of the room. Cherry didn't seem to notice, or if she did, she didn't care. She leaned back, letting her hair fall over her shoulders, her lips curving into a practiced smile.

Mike's heart pounded as he watched her through the lens. This was it—the beginning of his new film. A different kind of story. He didn't know where it would go, didn't know if it would end the way Forbidden Fruit had, with blood and despair. But that was the beauty of it. The unpredictability.

"Are you going to just watch?" Cherry teased, her voice breaking through his thoughts.

Mike blinked, snapping out of his reverie. He moved towards her, his fingers fumbling with the buttons of his shirt. The camera whirred softly in the background, capturing every movement, every breath.

This wasn't about lust or desire. It wasn't even about Cherry. It was about filling the emptiness, about chasing a ghost through the neon-lit streets of Bangkok. About finding a piece of himself that had shattered long ago.

As Cherry's laughter filled the room, Mike felt a strange sense of calm settle over him. He was back where it had all started—back in the city that had both made and destroyed him.

And this time, he wouldn't let it go so easily.

Chapter 20: A New Script

The room was dim, the only light emanating from the laptop screen perched on the desk. Mike leaned back in his chair, a glass of whisky in his hand, as he clicked through the footage. The images played out in front of him: Cherry's soft smile as she peeled off her clothes, his own dispassionate face reflected in the mirror, their bodies intertwined on the cheap hotel bed.

He had watched it all a dozen times now, but each viewing left him more disappointed than the last. There was no thrill, no rush. Just a sterile series of movements, devoid of meaning or excitement. He fast-forwarded through the clip, his eyes narrowing as Cherry's face contorted in faux ecstasy.

"Boring," he muttered, clicking the pause button. He drained his glass, the alcohol burning his throat. What was it that made Forbidden Fruit so... compelling? Why did he feel that surge of satisfaction editing that film, but not this?

The answer was simple. the element of the forbidden. Minow had been unaware, oblivious to his lens capturing her every vulnerable moment. That's what made it real, what made it exciting. Cherry, on the other hand, knew exactly what was happening, her movements carefully choreographed. He needed to recapture that rawness, that authenticity.

Mike closed his laptop with a snap, the screen going dark. He ran a hand through his hair, staring at his reflection in the blank screen. What now?

He turned his gaze to the corner of the room, where the small GoPro sat on its tripod, positioned in front of the bathroom door. That was the next step. He'd film from outside, catching glimpses of someone doing something personal—intimate. A girl shaving, vulnerable and exposed, with no idea he was watching. The thought sent a shiver down his spine.

But who?

The question echoed in his mind as he slipped on his jacket and grabbed his wallet. He needed a new actress, someone who would play her part without asking too many questions. As he stepped out into the humid Bangkok night, the answer seemed obvious: Soi Cowboy.

A short taxi ride later, and he was standing at the entrance of the narrow, neon-lit alley. The bar girls, draped in tight outfits that left little to the imagination, lined the sidewalks, their voices overlapping in a cacophony of invitations. He scanned the faces, looking for something different, something that would fit the part he was casting.

He walked slowly, his eyes flicking from one girl to the next. Most of them smiled back, beckoning him over with a wave or a flutter of fingers. He ignored them. They were too eager, too polished. He needed someone less polished, someone who still had a hint of innocence about her. Someone who would look unsure, hesitant.

"Hey, handsome!" A girl with heavy makeup and a plunging neckline reached out to grab his arm, but he brushed past her, shaking his head.

He stopped in front of a small bar at the far end of the alley, where a group of girls were huddled together, talking quietly. One of them caught his eye—a petite girl with long, black hair cascading down her back. She was dressed simply, in a tight-fitting tank top and shorts, her face free of the heavy makeup that caked the others. She stood slightly apart from the group, her gaze distant, almost disinterested.

Perfect.

Mike stepped inside the bar, his eyes never leaving the girl. He ordered a beer, then nodded in her direction. The mamasan, a stout woman with a wide smile, gestured for the girl to come over.

"Hello, I'm Nuan," she said softly, her voice barely audible over the thumping music. She shifted her weight from one foot to the other, avoiding his gaze.

Mike smiled, trying to put her at ease. "Nuan, would you like to join me for a drink?"

She nodded, slipping onto the stool beside him. They exchanged the usual pleasantries, but Mike kept the conversation light. He didn't want to scare her off. After a few rounds of drinks, she seemed more relaxed, her shoulders loosening, a shy smile curving her lips.

"You look like you could use a break," Mike said casually, his tone light. "I have a place nearby. We could go there, just talk. I promise nothing... heavy."

Nuan hesitated, her eyes searching his face. He held her gaze, keeping his expression open, honest.

"Okay," she whispered finally.

They left the bar together, slipping into a taxi. Mike's heart pounded in his chest, anticipation thrumming through his veins. This was it—the start of his new project. He didn't speak during the ride, letting Nuan's nerves simmer as she glanced out the window. When they arrived at his hotel, she followed him inside, her steps slow and deliberate.

The room was just as he'd left it, the GoPro still discreetly positioned. He guided her inside, offering her a seat on the bed.

"Would you like to freshen up?" he asked, gesturing towards the bathroom.

Nuan nodded, her gaze flicking nervously to the closed door. "Yes, please."

"Take your time," Mike said, his voice steady. "There's everything you need— shampoo, soap… even a razor if you want to shave."

She blinked, a frown creasing her forehead. "Shave?"

"Yeah," Mike said casually. "It's just a suggestion. You know, make yourself comfortable." He forced a smile. "I'll wait out here."

Nuan hesitated, then slowly stood and made her way to the bathroom. Mike waited until he heard the soft click of the door before he moved, adjusting the GoPro slightly, making sure the angle was right. He slipped out of his shirt, positioning himself near the door so that the camera would catch him peeking through the narrow crack.

The water started running, and he held his breath. The thrill of anticipation coursed through him as he imagined what was happening behind that door. He'd film her, capture her in her most private moment. And then, he'd catch himself, the voyeur, watching from the shadows.

His fingers tightened around the camera's remote. This would be his masterpiece. The film that brought everything full circle. He didn't know if it would end with blood in the bath, like Forbidden Fruit. But that was the beauty of it—the unpredictability.

Chapter 21: The Thin Line Between Art and Obscenity

The accolades rolled in like a tidal wave, sweeping Mike into a realm of acclaim he had never imagined. He sat in his small home office, the walls lined with the awards and certificates that bore witness to his controversial success. The latest email on his screen was from the Berlin International Film Festival, confirming Forbidden Fruit had won Best Short Film, yet again. That made it six wins in four months, with prestigious titles from Tokyo, Germany, Italy, India, and even the UK.

But as he scrolled through congratulatory messages from film critics and festival coordinators, a hollow sensation gnawed at him. He took a deep breath, staring at the blinking cursor on the empty document labelled Screenplay: New Project. The words wouldn't come. Everything felt inadequate, flat.

How could he follow up something as raw and personal as Forbidden Fruit? The film had been visceral, capturing Minow's final days through a lens of unspeakable intimacy and pain. It was a film that blurred the lines between documentary and art, earning him both praise and controversy. It was also the last footage of her—Minow's body, lifeless and submerged in the bathwater-stained red. He'd never shown that scene, of course.

He'd edited it out, cutting to black right before her pale fingers slipped beneath the surface.

But the memory of it haunted him. And it haunted the viewers too, who'd never quite known how close to the edge the film had come. Mike's name was whispered in dark corners of the film community, the question on everyone's lips: Was it real? Did she die for his art?

Now, he was wondering something even darker. Could he make a movie where the final scene did end in death? Was that too far? Would it be obscene, crossing the boundary into exploitation, or worse snuff?

He swirled the whisky in his glass, staring at the amber liquid. Was it art if you crossed that line knowingly, deliberately? Or did the awareness taint it, turning it into something grotesque?

"Art," he muttered aloud, a derisive smile twisting his lips. "What a load of bullshit."

He stood up, pacing the small room. His gaze landed on the awards on the wall. Tokyo, Berlin, Rome, Mumbai, London— every one of them applauding his vision, his boldness. But none of them knew what it really took, what he'd had to do to make something worthy of their applause. None of them had been there when he held Minow's limp body, the warmth leaving her as he stood in the bathroom, his camera rolling.

The lines between art and reality had blurred, and now he was left standing on the precipice. What would be his next masterpiece? How could he possibly top Forbidden Fruit?

Mike moved to the desk, opening his laptop. He clicked through some of the comments left on the private Vimeo account where he'd posted the film for festivals to review. There were the usual praises for the film's raw honesty, its "harrowing portrayal of a woman's descent into madness." But a few comments caught his eye.

One reviewer from India had written: The ending is abrupt—almost too clean. It leaves the viewer with an unsettling feeling of incompletion. As if there's more to the story we're not seeing.

Another critic from Germany had remarked: The lack of finality in the narrative arc felt deliberate, as if the filmmaker was holding back. This is a film that hints at the forbidden but pulls back at the last moment. Was that an artistic choice, or a failure of courage?

Mike leaned back in his chair, a slow smile spreading across his face. Maybe they were right. Maybe Forbidden Fruit had pulled its punch. Maybe there was more he needed to show, more he needed to reveal to complete the story.

But how far could he go before it became something else entirely?

He opened a new document and typed out the title: Concept: Final Cut. He stared at the screen for a long moment, his fingers hovering over the keys. Then he began to type, the words spilling out faster than his thoughts could keep up.

FADE IN:

INT. BATHROOM - NIGHT

The camera is positioned outside the door, peeking through a crack. A woman's silhouette is visible in the dim light, her back to the camera. She is leaning over the sink, her shoulders shaking as if she's sobbing. The camera zooms in slowly, capturing the quiver of her exposed skin.

He stopped, taking a deep breath. His fingers itched to type more, to build the scene until it reached its inevitable climax. But what was that climax?

He turned the idea over in his mind. There were two options, really. One: he found an actress, someone willing to go to the edge, to play a role so convincingly that the audience couldn't tell if it was real or not. Or two: he crossed the line for real. He filmed the scene as he'd filmed Minow—

capturing the moment where art and life collided in one final, irreversible act.

Mike felt a thrill run through him at the thought. The critics had hinted that Forbidden Fruit had pulled back, and they were right. He had held back. But what if he didn't? What if he showed everything? What if he filmed a death that no one could question, a performance so authentic that the world couldn't look away?

He knew what people called it when someone did that—a snuff film. But was it really a snuff film if the subject was willing? If it was staged, performed, with consent?

He shook his head. It was all semantics. The labels didn't matter. What mattered was the art. The vision.

Mike clicked off the laptop and stood up, feeling the adrenaline course through him. He knew what he had to do. The idea for his next film was crystallizing in his mind. All he needed now was to find the right person, someone who would fit the role perfectly.

He glanced at the empty suitcase by the door, still half-packed from his trip. He was in the right place to find what he needed. Bangkok was full of lost souls, people willing to do anything for a chance at money, fame, or just a way out.

All he had to do was go back out there and look.

One night in Bangkok. That's all it would take. He'd find her, and when he did, he'd make his final masterpiece.

A film that no one would ever forget. A film that would leave the world questioning the very nature of art and morality.

And maybe, just maybe, it would finally satisfy the darkness inside him that had been growing ever since Minow's death.

Chapter 22: The Next Scene

Mike's fingers tightened around the small wad of cash as he glanced up at the girl standing in front of him. She had just finished in the bathroom, her skin still glistening with a faint sheen of moisture. Her black hair was swept to one side, revealing the smooth, bare skin of her neck and collarbone. The room was silent, save for the steady hum of the air conditioning.

He took a deep breath, his gaze dropping to the cash in his hand before he stepped forward, holding it out. She looked at him quizzically, her eyes dark and unblinking.

"Here," he said quietly. "For you."

She didn't move at first, her gaze shifting between the money and his face. He forced a smile, tilting his head slightly. "It's just a bonus… for helping me out with this next scene. There's more if you're willing to do one more thing for me."

Her eyes flickered, a small smile curving her lips. Slowly, she reached out and took the money, letting it rest on her open palm for a moment before curling her fingers around it.

"What do you want me to do?" Her voice was soft, almost curious.

Mike cleared his throat, turning away to grab the screenplay he'd been working on from his desk. He flipped it open, tapping the page with a finger as he held it out to her.

"Just a scene," he murmured. "I'll pay you well. It's nothing difficult. You'll just be… reading."

The girl tilted her head, glancing down at the screenplay before looking back up at him. She hesitated, then shrugged. "Okay."

She wrapped the towel around her body more securely and followed Mike to the small desk by the hotel room's window. He pulled out the chair for her, gesturing for her to sit. She complied, adjusting the towel around her as she settled in.

Mike moved back a few steps, positioning himself just behind the small GoPro camera set up on a tripod. He leaned down, adjusting the angle slightly before nodding to himself. Perfect. He clicked on the camera, the small red light blinking to life.

"Alright," he said softly. "Just read the lines on the page. Don't worry about memorizing it. Just… read. And remember, you're curious. You're intrigued by what you're seeing."

The girl nodded, flipping open the first page of the screenplay. As she began to read, Mike's gaze shifted to her body, watching as she adjusted her position, the towel slipping slightly from her shoulders. He kept his face neutral, forcing himself to remain focused on the task at hand.

This was just the beginning. He needed to set the stage, build the atmosphere. The tension. The anticipation.

He picked up his phone, glancing at the notes he'd scribbled down earlier, before looking back up at the girl.

"Let the towel slip a little," he instructed quietly. "Just a little… like it's accidental. Don't look up. Keep reading."

The girl glanced up at him briefly, a faint smile on her lips, before turning her attention back to the screenplay. She shifted in her seat, her hands loosening their grip on the towel as she leaned forward slightly. The fabric slipped, revealing more of her bare skin.

Mike felt a thrill run through him, his gaze fixed on the camera's viewfinder. This was what he'd been missing in his previous attempts—the raw, unfiltered intimacy. The sense of vulnerability.

"Perfect," he murmured, his voice barely audible. "Now… read the opening scene. Just let it flow."

SCREENPLAY: "Final Cut"

INT. HOTEL ROOM - NIGHT

The camera is positioned in the corner of the room, capturing the soft glow of a lamp casting a pool of warm light over a modest desk. A young woman, mid-twenties, sits at the desk, her damp hair cascading over one shoulder. She's wrapped in a bath towel, the fabric barely clinging to her skin. She is alone in the room, a screenplay opened in front of her. She reads aloud, her voice soft, almost uncertain.

GIRL

(reading from the screenplay)

"When I close my eyes, I can still hear his voice. The way he whispered my name… as if he owned me. I thought… I thought I could escape. But some things… some people… they follow you."

She pauses, glancing down at her exposed shoulder. The towel slips further, revealing the soft curve of her breast, but she doesn't react. She's too focused on the words.

GIRL

(reading on)

"Maybe it's fate. Maybe it's punishment. I don't know. All I know is that I'm here now… and I can't get away."

The camera zooms in, focusing on the tension in her posture—the way her fingers tremble slightly as she grips the edge of the script. The room is silent, save for the sound of her breathing.

GIRL

(whispering)

"I wish… I wish I could go back. I wish I'd never met him."

She looks up, as if sensing someone is watching her. The camera holds on her gaze, capturing the flicker of fear in her eyes.

Mike watched her read, his fingers tightening around the edges of the desk as she moved through the scene. She was good. Maybe too good. There was something almost unsettling about the way she inhabited the role, her expression shifting seamlessly between fear, regret, and something darker—something that hinted at desire.

As she finished the last line, she let out a soft sigh, closing the screenplay and leaning back in the chair. The towel slipped further, exposing more of her chest.

"Is that okay?" she asked, glancing up at him.

Mike swallowed hard, his throat dry. He nodded, forcing himself to smile. "Yeah. That was perfect."

He turned off the camera, moving around the desk to stand in front of her. He reached out, brushing a loose strand of hair away from her face. She didn't flinch, just looked up at him with those same dark, curious eyes.

"There's more, you know," he said softly. "If you want to be a part of this... there's more to the story. But it's not for everyone. It's... intense."

The girl tilted her head, considering him for a long moment. Then she smiled—a slow, almost predatory smile.

"I'm not afraid of intense," she murmured. "Show me what comes next."

Mike's pulse quickened, the thrill of anticipation coursing through him. This was it. He could feel it. The beginning of something new, something darker than anything he'd ever attempted before.

He leaned down, placing his hands on either side of her, his voice dropping to a whisper.

"Be careful what you wish for," he murmured, his breath warm against her ear. "Sometimes, the script writes itself… and sometimes, it doesn't have a happy ending."

The girl's smile widened, her gaze never wavering.

"Good," she whispered back. "Happy endings are boring."

Mike straightened, staring down at her. He could see it in her eyes—the willingness.

The curiosity. The need for something more. And he knew, in that moment, that he'd found his next star.

The scene was set. Now, it was time to see where the story would lead.

Chapter 23: Pushing Boundaries

Mike sat alone in his Bangkok hotel room, the dim glow of the city's neon lights filtering through the heavy curtains. He looked down at the small plastic bag in his hand, its contents casting a faint, ominous shadow on the table before him. The bag contained a fine white powder—something he had gone to great lengths to acquire. The drug was commonly known as the 'Date Rape' drug. Its effects? Lethargy, confusion, and a deep, unnatural sleep. The idea had been gnawing at the back of his mind ever since he'd started conceptualizing the next film.

But it was only an idea until now. Could he really do this? Could he push the boundaries of his art even further?

The girl from the other night—Nuen—had been a good start. She was beautiful, willing, but something had been missing from the footage. He needed more than just willing compliance; he needed realism. Something raw and unfiltered. He needed to control the scene, every moment, every breath.

Mike's hands trembled slightly as he set the bag down on the table. He stared at it, his mind racing with possibilities. He could film her looking weak, frail, like life itself was slipping away. He could capture the very essence of helplessness. With the drug, she'd be too lethargic to fight back, too disoriented to question what he was doing.

And she wouldn't remember a thing.

He stood abruptly, pacing the length of the room. His mind was a whirlwind of thoughts, doubts, and excitement. He could film her in a state of total vulnerability, record every moment of her struggle to keep her eyes open, to move, to speak. And when she finally gave in to the drug's effects, he could shape the scene to show a slow descent into unconsciousness.

He could create a visual metaphor for death itself, without ever crossing the line.

"Is it too far?" he whispered to himself, stopping to stare at his own reflection in the mirror. He saw his eyes—wide, almost feverish. The man staring back at him was unrecognizable. He wasn't the same person who had flown to Thailand with Minow's ashes only a few weeks ago.

This was someone else. Someone driven by a need that went beyond mere filmmaking.

Mike walked back to the table, picking up the bag once more. His thumb traced over the edge of the seal, contemplating. Nuan had been more than happy to take the money last night. Would she be as willing tonight? He could tell her it was just to help her relax for the next scene. Just something to take the edge off.

She'd believe him. They all did.

He pulled out his phone and scrolled through his contacts until he found her name. After a moment's hesitation, he pressed 'call' and waited. It rang twice before she picked up, her voice soft and inviting.

"Hello?"

"Nuan, it's me, Mike. I've got another role for you, if you're interested. It's a little more... challenging than the last one."

There was a brief pause on the other end, then the sound of soft laughter. "Challenging, huh? How much are we talking?"

Mike smiled, his grip tightening around the phone. "Double what I paid you last time. And there's a bonus if you really give it your all."

Another pause, longer this time. Then: "Alright. I'm interested. When do we start?"

"Tonight. I'll send a car to pick you up in an hour. Just be ready to relax and follow my direction, okay?"

"Got it. See you soon."

Mike hung up, the weight of his decision settling heavily in his chest. He placed the phone back on the table next to the bag of powder. He stared at them both for what felt like an eternity before moving to the desk and pulling out a small notepad. He began scribbling notes, outlining the new scene with precise, careful details.

Screenplay Outline: "The Descent"

INT. HOTEL ROOM - NIGHT

The camera captures Nuan lying on the bed, her body limp, eyes half-closed. She's still wearing the loose-fitting white dress from earlier, but now it clings to her skin as if she's been sweating. She's breathing shallowly, her lips parting slightly as if to speak, but no words come out.

Mike's shadow crosses the frame as he stands over her, his hand reaching out to brush a strand of hair from her face.

MIKE

(voice-over)

"This is the moment where everything changes. When the world fades away, and all that's left is you... and the darkness."

The camera cuts to a close-up of Nuan's face. Her eyelids flutter, struggling to stay open. She tries to lift a hand, but it falls back to her side, useless. A small, almost imperceptible smile forms on her lips—whether from the drug or a genuine reaction, it's impossible to tell.

Mike's hand enters the frame again, this time holding the camera at a low angle, looking down at her. His voice is calm, almost soothing.

MIKE

"Just let go. Let everything slip away."

The camera shifts, capturing the moment she finally closes her eyes, her body sinking deeper into the bed. The light above casts a harsh glow, accentuating the shadows on her face. The frame holds on her still form, the silence in the room heavy and suffocating.

Mike set the notepad down, his heart pounding. He could see it so clearly now. The way the light would catch the sheen of sweat on her skin. The way her breathing would slow, becoming more and more shallow. He would film her struggle against the drug's effects, the way her body would fight to stay conscious.

And when she finally succumbed, he would capture that moment—the exact second when she gave in and fell into darkness.

But that last scene... the one that had haunted his thoughts ever since he'd started planning this film...

The scene where Nuan lay lifeless in the bath, the water stained red, her eyes open but empty.

Could he do it? Could he take it that far?

The line between art and depravity was thin, almost invisible. He had danced along it for so long, but this… this was something else. Something darker. He felt his stomach twist at the thought, but he couldn't deny the excitement coursing through him.

The film festivals had loved his last project. They had called it daring, visionary. They had praised his ability to capture the human condition in such an unflinching way.

Would they praise this too? Would they see the art in it, the beauty in capturing the end of a life on film?

Mike looked at the small bag of powder once more, his decision hanging in the balance. He reached out, picking it up, and slipped it into his pocket. His fingers brushed against the GoPro camera, and he closed his eyes, taking a deep breath.

This was it. The beginning of something that would either define him as a filmmaker—or destroy him completely.

He stood, his gaze hardening as he grabbed his phone and wallet. He had a girl to meet, a scene to direct.

And a story to tell that the world would never forget.

Chapter 24: Crossing the Line

Mike leaned back in his chair; his eyes fixed on the laptop screen in front of him. The footage from the night before played silently, Nuan's body illuminated in soft light, her skin glowing under the lens. There was an undeniable grace in her movements, even though she was unaware of being filmed. A pang of guilt shot through him, but he pushed it aside.

It wasn't about exploitation, he told himself. This was art. His art.

The door to the room clicked softly as he shut it, sealing himself away from the outside world. The dim glow of the city beyond the windows cast long shadows across the floor. He paused the video and stared at the frozen image of Nuan's face, her lips slightly parted, her expression caught between confusion and relaxation. The drug had taken hold quickly, as expected. But there was a look in her eyes— something Mike hadn't seen in any of his previous subjects. Trust? Fear? He couldn't tell.

This was a crossroads. Nuan had taken the money, she had agreed to play the role he'd described, but this—this was different. The power was entirely in his hands now, and he knew it. The excitement he'd once felt—the thrill of capturing the raw and unfiltered— now mixed with a sense of dread. What would come next? How far could he push this?

How far would he push it?

The door to the room cracked open, and Mike turned to see Nuan standing there. She wore the same loose-fitting T-shirt and shorts from the night before. Her eyes, though still dulled from the drug, met his. She smiled, a small, timid expression that made Mike's heart lurch. The film hadn't shattered her trust. Not yet.

"Are you filming today?" she asked, her voice soft and unsure.

Mike swallowed, his throat dry. He nodded, a slow, deliberate motion. "Yes. If you're feeling up to it."

Nuan's gaze drifted to the GoPro camera on the table beside him. "What's the scene?" she asked, a hint of curiosity lacing her tone.

Mike considered her for a moment, his fingers tapping lightly against the edge of the table. He could tell her the truth. He could say that he wanted to film her in a state of utter vulnerability, that he wanted to capture the descent into unconsciousness. He could describe the script he'd written, the way she would lay in the bath, the way the camera would follow her as the water turned red.

But he didn't.

"Something simple," he said instead, his voice even. "Just you… relaxing. Nothing too heavy. We can keep it light today."

Nuan nodded, her smile widening slightly. "Okay. Whatever you want."

She turned and walked back into the adjoining room, leaving the door ajar. Mike watched her go, his mind racing. He reached into his pocket and pulled out the small plastic bag. His hand trembled slightly as he placed it on the desk, staring at it like it was a loaded gun.

He could stop now. He could turn off the camera, let Nuan leave, and go back to his life. He didn't need to make this film.

But the allure was too strong. The praise from critics, the acclaim—he needed more. He needed to show the world what he could do, to push the boundaries even further. And Nuan… she was the perfect subject.

He rose from his chair and walked to the bathroom, the GoPro in hand. He adjusted the camera angle, making sure it captured the entire room. Then he returned to the desk, picking up the bag of powder. He stared at it, his pulse pounding in his ears.

Would she notice if he added a little more?

He carefully measured out a small dose, the white powder falling silently into a glass of water. He swirled it around, watching as it dissolved completely. Then, with a deep breath, he carried the glass into the bathroom where Nuan was waiting.

"Here," he said, offering her the glass. "Drink this. It'll help you relax."

Nuan took the glass without hesitation, her fingers brushing against his. She brought it to her lips and drank deeply, emptying the glass in one go. Mike watched, a strange mixture of relief and guilt flooding through him. She handed the glass back to him, her eyes already growing heavy.

"What's the next scene?" she asked, her words slightly slurred.

"Just lie down," Mike said gently, guiding her toward the bath. "Take a moment to yourself."

Nuan nodded, her movements slow and deliberate. She stepped into the bath, the water sloshing softly around her ankles. Mike adjusted the camera, making sure it was focused on her. The script he'd written played out in his mind—every shot, every angle, every line of dialogue. This was it. The scene he'd been waiting for.

"Close your eyes," he whispered, his voice barely audible over the sound of the running water.

Nuan's eyelids fluttered, then slowly closed. Her body relaxed, sinking deeper into the warm water. Mike stood at the edge of the bath, his breath catching in his throat. He reached out, brushing his fingers lightly against her cheek. She didn't stir.

This was the moment. The descent. The point where everything blurred—art, reality, life, and death.

He adjusted the camera one last time, making sure it captured every detail. He leaned over her, his voice a soft murmur.

"Just let go, Nuan. Let everything slip away."

For a moment, time seemed to stand still. Mike watched, his heart hammering in his chest, as Nuan's breathing slowed. Her lips parted, a faint, almost imperceptible sound escaping them. The water around her rippled softly, the light casting strange patterns across her skin.

And then, she was still.

Mike stared down at her, his mind a chaotic mess of thoughts and emotions. He'd done it. He'd captured the scene exactly as he'd imagined it. But as he stood there, looking at

Nuan's lifeless form, a cold, hollow feeling settled in his chest.

What had he done?

The camera continued to record, the red light blinking softly in the corner of the screen. Mike reached out, his fingers trembling as he turned it off. The room fell silent, the only sound the faint drip of water from the tap.

He backed away, his gaze never leaving Nuan. She looked peaceful, almost serene. But something was wrong. The sense of accomplishment he'd expected—the thrill of creating something truly unique—was absent. All he felt was emptiness.

And fear.

He glanced at the GoPro in his hand, then back at Nuan. This was supposed to be just another film. Just another project. But as he stood there, alone in the silence, he realized he'd crossed a line he could never come back from.

Slowly, he turned and left the bathroom, closing the door behind him. He walked back to the desk and sat down, his hands shaking as he placed the GoPro beside the laptop. He stared at the blank screen, his thoughts a jumbled mess.

What now?

The bag of powder lay on the desk, a reminder of how far he'd gone. He reached out, his fingers brushing against it. He could end it all now—destroy the footage, leave Nuan to wake up alone and confused. He could make it all disappear.

But he didn't.

Instead, he picked up the camera and began reviewing the footage, his eyes glued to the screen. The film played out exactly as he'd imagined it. Every shot, every angle, every expression. It was perfect.

But as he watched Nuan's still form, a cold realization settled in his chest.

Perfection had a price.

And he'd just paid it.

Chapter 25: A Line Crossed

Mike stood in the dimly lit bathroom, his breath catching as he saw Nuan's head submerged beneath the water. For a moment, time seemed to freeze. The water, which had once been calm, now seemed eerily still, disturbed only by the gentle rise of her hair, floating around her like a dark halo. He stared, his heart pounding in his chest, unsure if this was still part of the plan.

His mind raced, the adrenaline mixing with a cold sense of dread. He had given her the drug, filmed the perfect shot—captured the vulnerability, the helplessness. But now, staring at Nuan's motionless form, a sudden realization hit him: this wasn't part of the film. This wasn't art anymore.

A sharp ringing echoed through the hotel room, snapping him out of his stupor. It was Nuan's phone, vibrating insistently on the bedside table in the next room. The sound pierced the tension, making Mike flinch. His eyes darted from Nuan's submerged body to the door. For a brief second, he hesitated.

The camera was still running.

With shaking hands, he turned off the GoPro. The weight of the situation pressed down on him, a suffocating realization that the camera had recorded something far beyond what he'd planned. That was the closing scene. It had to be.

He rushed out of the bathroom, leaving Nuan behind, her lifeless form still floating in the water. The phone continued to ring. It felt like a countdown ticking away, a race against time he didn't know how to win.

Mike reached for the phone, silencing the insistent buzzing with a single swipe. The name on the screen, written in Thai, meant nothing to him. It was just another interruption. Another distraction.

His mind reeled. Nuan was gone. Just like that. Turned off. Like the phone in his hand. But now what?

The room fell silent again, the weight of his actions pressing on his chest. He sank into the bed, the phone still clutched tightly in his hand. Thoughts whirled in his head. How had this gone so far? When had his twisted pursuit of art led him to this moment?

The bathroom door stood ajar, a sliver of dim light spilling into the room. He could see the edge of the bath from where he sat, the water still shimmering faintly under the flickering fluorescent light. The horror of it all began to settle in, tightening his throat.

What was he going to do?

For the first time in years, Mike felt completely out of control. He had always been able to orchestrate the details of his life—his films, his encounters—but this was different. He had crossed a line. And now, staring at the door, he knew there was no way back.

His gaze drifted to the GoPro sitting on the desk. The footage was all there. The story, the perfect ending. The acclaim he sought, the attention, all hinged on that final moment. The closing shot of Nuan submerged in the red-tinged water.

Could he use it?

No. The thought was too monstrous, even for him.

Mike stood up, forcing himself to move. His legs felt heavy, as though weighed down by the enormity of what he had done. He walked slowly toward the bathroom, every step making his stomach churn.

He pushed the door open and knelt beside the bath, staring down at Nuan's lifeless face just beneath the surface. Her eyes were closed, her expression peaceful, as if she had simply fallen asleep. He reached out, his fingers trembling, and lifted her head from the water.

Her skin was cold.

Mike cradled her in his arms, the water dripping from her body onto the tiled floor. His breath came in shallow gasps, and the realization of what he had done finally hit him. Nuan wasn't a character in one of his films. She wasn't part of a scene. She was real, and now she was dead.

The ringing of the phone had stopped, leaving only the sound of water dripping from Nuan's limp body. Mike stood there, holding her, unsure of what to do next. He wanted to call someone, but who? He could erase the footage, pretend this never happened. But how could he explain Nuan's body?

The answer was simple: he couldn't.

He laid her down gently in the bath, her face tilted toward him as if she were still looking up at him with trust. He swallowed hard, his mind racing for solutions. But nothing came.

He wiped his hands on the towel, feeling the slickness of the water and blood on his palms. His breath grew shallow, panic setting in. His thoughts turned to the footage. It had to be erased. He couldn't leave any trace of this. No one could ever see it.

But as he reached for the GoPro, a cold wave of dread washed over him. What if someone had already seen it? What if this footage became more than just his private obsession?

Mike's hand hovered over the camera. He couldn't bring himself to delete it. Not yet. He had to think. He had to be smart about this. Turning away from Nuan's lifeless form in the bathroom, he sat on the bed, staring at the GoPro and the phone. The weight of his choices bore down on him.

He had always thought he could control everything—manipulate reality for the sake of art. But now, sitting in that cold, silent room, he realized how little control he truly had.

What would he do now?

What could he do?

Mike stared at the phone in his hand, the name on the screen still visible. He knew one thing: nothing would ever be the same again.

And he had no one to blame but himself.

Chapter 26: The Final Scene

The bathroom was filled with an eerie silence, the kind that seeps into your bones and takes hold, refusing to let go. Mike stood by the tub, staring at the body lying still in the water. Nuan's skin, once warm and alive, had taken on a deathly pallor. Her eyes were closed now, her face a picture of unsettling serenity.

He glanced at the camera perched on the counter—the GoPro that had captured it all. The red light blinked steadily, a small, unblinking eye that recorded everything without judgment. It would witness this too. His final scene.

There was no way out. He had known that the moment he'd dialled emergency services. They'd arrive soon, sirens blaring, doors crashing open. And they'd find everything: Nuan's body, the camera, and all the footage. He couldn't erase it all. He couldn't explain it away. He was cornered.

The thought of spending the rest of his life rotting away in a Thai prison chilled him to his core. The "Bangkok Hilton"—the notorious hellhole he'd heard stories about from expats and locals alike. He imagined himself in a cramped cell, suffocating in the oppressive heat, the stench of sweat and desperation clinging to his skin. It would be a slow death, far worse than anything he could have ever scripted for his films.

No. He wouldn't let them take him. He wouldn't give them that satisfaction. This was his story, and he would end it on his own terms.

With slow, deliberate movements, Mike turned away from the tub and walked to the small desk by the bathroom door. A small plastic bag sat there, filled with a fine, white powder—the remainder of the drug he'd used on Nuan. The powder had rendered her lethargic, pliable, and eventually, lifeless.

He picked up the bag, staring at it as if it held all the answers. A part of him marvelled at how something so small, so seemingly insignificant, could destroy lives. Could end them.

"This is it," he murmured, his voice hollow.

With careful precision, he emptied the contents of the bag onto the desk, forming a small pile of white dust. He scooped up the powder, dividing it into two lines. He'd need more than Nuan had taken. Enough to numb everything, to stop his heart, to let him slip away into the darkness without feeling a thing.

Mike stripped off his clothes, letting them fall in a crumpled heap on the floor. He looked at his reflection in the bathroom mirror, naked and vulnerable. There was no fear, no panic—just a strange, detached calm. This was how it would end.

He walked back to the tub, stepping carefully over the slick tiles. Nuan's body lay there, a silent companion in his final moments. He climbed in beside her, shivering as the cold water embraced him. Her skin brushed against his own, icy and unyielding.

He sat there for a moment, letting the reality of it sink in. Then, with trembling fingers, he reached for the razor blade he'd left on the edge of the tub. The thin steel glinted under the fluorescent light, sharp and unforgiving.

"It's all part of the movie," he whispered, almost to reassure himself. "Every good film needs a dramatic ending."

He drew the blade across his forearm, just deep enough to break the skin. A thin line of blood welled up, dark and vivid against his pale skin. He watched as it trickled down, mixing with the water, blooming like a crimson flower.

Again, he cut. And again. He switched arms, slicing deeper this time, feeling a dull sting. The water around him turned a murky red, the blood swirling in delicate tendrils.

He set the blade down beside him and reached over to the GoPro. With a flick of his finger, he pressed play and then record. The red light blinked back at him, capturing his final act.

Mike took a deep breath and submerged himself beneath the water, his head sliding down beside Nuan's. His world became a blur of red and white, his ears filled with the muted sound of his own heartbeat. It was strangely peaceful.

His lungs began to burn, but he forced himself to stay under. He closed his eyes, feeling his body grow heavier, the water pulling him down. He reached out blindly, his fingers brushing against Nuan's cold hand. He held on tightly, letting himself drift.

Seconds stretched into eternity. The pain in his chest intensified, and his body fought instinctively to rise, to breathe. But he stayed under, refusing to give in. This was his choice. His ending.

The last thing he felt was the faint prickling of the drug taking hold, numbing his mind, lulling him into a state of blissful oblivion. His grip on Nuan's hand loosened, and he let go.

Above the water, the camera recorded the stillness. The two bodies, side by side, bathed in blood-red water. The room was silent, save for the faint hum of the camera.

And then, nothing.

The final scene. The perfect closing shot.

The camera blinked once more, its memory card full, before the red light faded, leaving the room in darkness.

Chapter 27: The Final Cut

It started with a nondescript package, mailed anonymously to a modest production company in the heart of Bangkok. Inside, wrapped in plain brown paper, was a single USB drive labelled Final Cut. No sender's name. No return address. Just that cryptic title.

Curiosity piqued, the production assistant slipped the drive into her laptop, expecting to find another amateur submission. Perhaps a poorly shot short film or a bizarre indie experiment, like so many that came through their doors. But as the video began to play, she quickly realized this was something different—something unsettling and compelling in equal measure.

The film opened with the familiar shaky shots of a Bangkok hotel room. The camera panned across ordinary objects—a cluttered desk, a small bathroom mirror, a bathtub. The audio was muted, the silence heavy, creating a sense of foreboding that was hard to shake. Then the scene shifted.

There was a woman—Thai, beautiful, with a haunting sadness in her eyes. She was reading a piece of paper, wrapped in a towel, her hair wet and tangled. As she moved, the towel slipped, revealing more of her skin. There was nothing pornographic about it, yet it exuded an uncomfortable intimacy, like peering through a keyhole into someone's private world.

The story unfolded slowly, in disjointed fragments. There were scenes of the woman showering, dressing, and performing mundane tasks—each filmed with a voyeuristic precision that made the viewer feel complicit. And then, abruptly, the mood darkened.

The final sequence showed the woman in a bathtub, her body partially submerged in dark, red-tinted water. A man's shadow appeared at the edge of the frame. He spoke softly, his words inaudible, his tone unsettlingly calm. The camera lingered on her lifeless form for an agonizingly long time before cutting to black.

The assistant watched in stunned silence as the credits rolled, a single name flashing across the screen: Michael Young. The piece ended with a dedication—For Nuan.

She forwarded it to her boss, who forwarded it to his contacts. Within days, the video had made its way up the chain, generating a wave of hushed conversations and heated debates. Was it a genuine piece of art, or something far more sinister? No one knew for sure, but it didn't matter. The film was captivating, disturbing, and, above all, unforgettable.

In a matter of weeks, Final Cut found itself on the radar of major film festivals. The Los Angeles Arthouse Film Critics praised it as "a raw exploration of voyeurism and obsession." In Berlin, it was described as "a bold, unflinching look at the dark side of human desire." Tokyo's Underground Cinema hailed it as "brilliantly subversive, blending reality and fiction in a way that leaves the audience questioning everything."

The controversy only fuelled its success. Audiences were drawn to the film's mystery, to the chilling ambiguity of its final scene. The man behind the camera—Michael Young—had vanished, his whereabouts unknown, leaving the world to speculate. Was it real? Was it staged? Did Final Cut depict an actual death, or was it merely a masterful piece of illusion?

Critics and audiences were split. Some called for the film to be banned, declaring it a dangerous glorification of violence. Others championed it as a groundbreaking work of art, a fearless dive into the murky waters of morality and mortality. Awards piled up, and the film's notoriety grew. It was whispered about in elite circles, dissected in academic papers, and banned in several countries for its ambiguous nature.

There were even rumours that the Thai authorities had launched an investigation into the identities of those involved. But with no concrete evidence, and no one stepping forward to claim responsibility, the case went cold. The movie remained an enigma—an unsolved riddle frozen in time.

Back in Bangkok, in a small, dimly lit office, the assistant who had first watched the film received a final email. It was from an untraceable address, signed simply M.Y.. Attached was a short message: "Thank you for sharing her story. She's home now."

The assistant stared at the message for a long time, her finger hovering over the delete key. She knew she should report it. She knew there were too many questions, too many loose ends. But in the end, she let it be.

She closed her laptop, leaving the office and stepping out into the bustling chaos of Sukhumvit. The world outside continued, indifferent to the film and its mysteries. Life moved on, unperturbed by the strange and tragic story of a woman named Nuan and the man who captured her final moments.

And somewhere, hidden deep within the labyrinthine streets of Bangkok, a camera blinked red, recording the city's restless pulse.

It was over.

But the film would live on.

Printed in Great Britain
by Amazon

48934037R00128